Prairie Schooner Book Prize in Fiction

EDITOR Kwame Dawes

Better Times

SHORT STORIES   *Sara Batkie*

WITHDRAWN

University of Nebraska Press | Lincoln and London

Library of Congress
Cataloging-in-Publication Data

Names: Batkie, Sara, author.
Title: Better times: short stories / Sara
Batkie.
Description: Lincoln: University of
Nebraska Press, [2018] | Series: Prairie
Schooner book prize in fiction
Identifiers: LCCN 2018014270
ISBN 9781496207876 (pbk.: alk. paper)
ISBN 9781496211958 (epub)
ISBN 9781496211965 (mobi)
ISBN 9781496211972 (pdf)
Classification: LCC PS3602.A8935 A6 2018
DDC 813/.6—dc23 LC record available at
https://urldefense.proofpoint.com/v2/url?u
=https-3a__lccn.loc.gov_2018014270&d=
Dwifag&c=Cu5g146wZdoqVuKptnsyhefx
_rg6kWhlklf8eft-wwo&r=
Qxk-cj_QrVzf1u7b7vxqTw
&m=wyf30jpffebGuoknN
_g7hhf6z-M_o2vde86astwdwsQ&s=Tix
_z0utecsuiimwGcx5lopdQbbf53ulwcyc2
_oS-q4&e=.

Set in Whitman by Mikala R Kolander.
Designed by L. Auten.

For Adina

Contents

Acknowledgments

Some stories in this book were over ten years in the writing and many people helped make them better along the way.

First I must thank the teachers without whose wisdom and encouragement I would not still be writing. Thanks to Katie Chase at the University of Iowa, for being the first to make me take myself seriously. To the amazing New York University brain trust of Brian Morton, Jonathan Lethem, Darin Strauss, and the dearly missed E. L. Doctorow: it was an honor beyond belief to be in your classrooms. To my fellow NYU students in the trenches, especially Tusia, Kimberly, and Dave: thank you for the late nights after workshop, when the A Train had already started going local but we needed to get in one more round of cheap beers at Treehouse. To Tanya, Miranda, and Caedra: my membership in our writing group was short-lived but your perceptiveness made me feel instantly welcomed and challenged.

To my UI Currier 04–05 crew, especially Alyssa, Molly, Danny, Tara, and honorary members Beth, Peter, and JJ: you were some of the first people I shared serious work with and you continue to inspire me daily. May our future hold more cakes and trips to Hoboken for cookie decorating and holiday brunches. Thanks also to Thais, for your early reads and remarkable insight. If page counts were medals I'd owe you several display cases worth.

To the incredible staff at *One Story*, who were the first to bring me into the fold of New York's big, scary literary world and show me how kind and generous it could be. Maribeth Batcha, Hannah Tinti, Patrick Ryan, Marie-Helene Bertino, Karen Friedman: I'd stuff envelopes for you anytime. To Amanda, Jesse, and Jenni: we waded through slush together and found lasting friendships. To Emily, Christine, Julia, and Seth: thank you for keeping the kindness and generosity train of NYC going. To my dearest Adina: I was so lucky to know you and will do my best to keep your singular brightness burning every day.

To my Center for Fiction people, who have become so much more than coworkers over our years together: Noreen Tomassi and Cal Morgan, it's an inspiration to see what you do every day for the literary world and I'm still awed I get to be even a small part of it. Kristin, Gwen, Elise, Rosie, Matt, Chris, Kris, Meghan, Jon, Amanda, and Sugar: when is that next happy hour meet-up? To all the immensely talented Emerging Writers I've had the privilege of meeting and working with through the Center's fellowship program: you're a big part of the reason I keep punching the clock.

To Kwame Dawes and Ashley Strosnider of *Prairie Schooner* and judges Christine Sneed and Chigozie Obioma: thank you for selecting this manuscript. To Courtney Ochsner and the rest of the staff at the University of Nebraska Press: thanks for helping usher it into the world. To Pat Friedli and everyone at the Kimmel Harding Nelson Center: thank you for offering such a serene space for artists. To Bill Henderson: thanks for seeing fit to honor "Laika" with a Pushcart Prize in 2017. And to the journals that first published the following stories:

Bellevue Literary Review, for "When Her Father Was an Island"
Epiphany, for "Those Who Left and Those Who Stayed"
Gulf Coast, for "Cleavage"
Michigan Quarterly Review, for "Foreigners"
New Orleans Review, for "Laika"

One Story, for "Departures"
Salt Hill, for "No Man's Land"

Last, but never, ever least: to my parents, Steve and Cathy Batkie, my earliest and most steadfast supporters; to my sister, Emily, my brother-in-law, Andrew, and their atomically adorable son, Teddy; and to my grandparents, Ed, Marilyn, Frank, and Carolyn, some of whom are no longer with us but are missed every day: I love you all. There would be no book without you. There would be no words without you.

Better Times

THE RECENT PAST

When Her Father Was an Island

In his dreams it was always a child who told him about the end of the war. From his perch high above the fields Father would watch as the figure approached, grass bending beneath its feet. A light mist would be falling and, as the child reached the guard tower, Father would turn his face up to the sky, close his eyes, and thank the emperor for allowing him to serve. He would awaken feeling refreshed, happy. If nobody came he was happier still. It meant he had not failed the emperor and the emperor had not failed the world. "Stay and fight," the emperor had told him, and that was what Father would do.

Maemi was two years old and being held in her mother's arms when she first heard her father was missing. Missing in action, she would learn. Presumed dead, she would learn even later. At the time she did not know any of this. She just felt her mother's heart breaking. The war had been over for six months by then. She did not know this either. But, it seemed, neither did he.

When Father signed up for the war, Mother was five-and-a-half months pregnant, their child roughly the size of a ripe pomegranate. She did not beg him not to go and he did not wish her to. They had the same understanding of duty. In those early days of the fighting, everyone did.

Father had always been a quiet man, but this did not make him a simple one, and during his intelligence training he was routinely singled out by his superiors as an exemplary officer. They called him "the Ghost" for his ability to sneak up on others. He was rumored to walk through walls. His was a country of mountains and valleys, all of them being ravaged. After a month of combat on the laced edges of the land, after grappling with attackers that came by sea, he was sent to an island jungle outpost with two others, a private and a lieutenant, where his quietness could be weaponized into stealth. Their operation was simple: ward off invaders in any way they could. The airstrip had been destroyed, the pier blasted into the sea. The isolation of the mission matched the strangeness of their surroundings. All civilians had been evacuated long ago. Only the rubber trees, weeping their gluey tears, remained while the soldiers waited for the emperor's divine word.

Maemi was growing up in a sorrowful house. Her mother wore her grief like a new skin. When she bathed Maemi she would often weep silently, a condition that terrified the girl. But it was also the only time her mother touched her, so she would dirty herself unnecessarily by making mudcakes in the yard or rolling about in the fireplace soot. "Worse than a mutt," her mother would say, but she would be tender with her, rubbing a soft cloth under her fingernails, dabbing at the shallow webs between her toes.

Once a week they would visit the temple in Nagoya and pray for her father's safe return. It was not a ritual that Maemi enjoyed. She hated the way their shoes clacked against the floor, signaling their arrival even if no one else was there. The silence was heavy enough to force them to their knees if they were not already on their way there. She tented her hands as her mother did, but thoughts floated through her head like clouds. Her father was a photograph to her, a family legend, a hoax. Or perhaps he was a ghost now, a vengeful spirit. When her mother lit the candle for the shrine, dragging a match along the wood until it sparked, Maemi imagined her father dancing in the flame, spinning and coiling until it built and billowed and swallowed whole the room around them. The first time she was allowed to light a candle by herself she cried.

Father had fallen in love with Mother's legs first. One day while walking past the pear tree fields he spotted a ladder and two long tapering limbs dangling under wispy ends of a skirt, the rest of the body lost among the leaves. The skirt was thin and yellow, as if the sun had been caught in its net. He watched a hand reach down and drop a piece of the fruit into a basket below. He moved to her side without her hearing and the next time the gesture was made he was there to take hold of her fingers. The air around them had the rumor of bees.

Father thought of her often while out in the bush. There was plenty of time. In the mornings he kept watch while his two men went into the wilderness to gather bananas and coconuts or to steal rice from the abandoned fields. Once a week they would sneak further out and kill any cattle that could be found, butchering and roasting the meat over a fire. They shied from the bramble of mosquitoes, patched their uniforms, and cleaned their rifles. At night, while the stars strung themselves together above, he lay down and lifted himself back into that tree, tasting the nectar that lived in the hollows of his beloved's skin.

When Maemi was eleven her mother found her a new father. One morning he was sitting at the kitchen table, sipping a cup of black tea, and then he never left. She was told to call him "Uncle," but that felt false on her tongue. He had no look of anyone she'd ever known. His hair was dark and tied in a long braid down his back. When he walked the braid swung like a metronome, keeping the music of time. One day, two days, one month, a year. She sat across from him and watched as he grew fat on their food. He called her "Mutton Chop" while wiping crumbs from his beard.

"Did you stop loving Father?" Maemi asked her mother.

"Of course not," Mother said. "But I cannot stay dutiful to a dead man."

When her mother and Uncle had been married a year, Maemi took down the only photograph of her father still remaining in the house. She slid it out from under the glass and moved her fingers over the glossy surface. His face was tinted green, his uniform pressed and snug. He held a rifle over his shoulder, like a soldier in a school textbook. He had no wrinkles, like her new father did, so she took a charcoal pencil and drew some in. Then she smudged hair onto his chin. From beneath his cap she snaked out a braid that fell over his left breast.

When Maemi was finished she hid the photograph under her bed. At night she whispered her secrets to it, recounted the events of her day. She kept waiting for her mother to ask where it had gone, but she never did.

The years were beginning to weigh the soldiers down like stones in a pocket. They had grown ragged and wild. Hair that once crept close to their scalps now brushed at their shoulders. Their clothes drooped from their bodies. But they built themselves huts and taught themselves songs and prayed for the safety and wisdom of the emperor.

One day the private and lieutenant returned from scavenging with a leaflet. Worn and sweat-stained, with frayed edges, it declared in bold red text the end of the war. A picture of the emperor was printed on it, his face hidden in his hands but recognizable nonetheless. "Where did you get this?" Father wanted to know, but they just shrugged and buried themselves in the crypts of their coats. "The enemy," he said, "is everywhere and can take many forms. We must be prepared. They wish to weaken our resolve. We must not let them."

But he, too, was shaken by the news. His mind passed over his wife and child, girl or boy he did not know. Were there invaders among them? Corrupting them? What would home look like now? Was there even any home to return to? That night Father tore the leaflet up and watched it dance upon the fire, the smoke rising to linger above the trees. Let them find us, he thought, so we may know them.

Maemi had trouble making friends at school. She had a reserved and forlorn nature that the other children had no patience to test. Her hair fell over her face in a black curtain and, when meeting the eyes of others, she had a tendency to blink rapidly until they looked away. She played solitary games in the courtyard; she made the television her confidant. She dreamed herself into worlds ruled by her words. At the dinner table her mother and Uncle talked around her. The fading photograph beneath her bed no longer seemed to be listening either.

She was sixteen before she knew the touch of a boy. He had a gentle but curious soul and was able to coax things from her that others couldn't. He would bring her pears from his parents' farm and cut them in halves to share, the insides of the fruit grainy and sweet. The first time he kissed her his spit melted on her tongue like sugar.

"What is your deepest fear?" he asked her one August evening. The sun was bowing over the horizon. She looked down at how her fingers laced through his, a cat's cradle of skin, and said, "That my father is still alive somewhere and has forgotten about me."

In the fall the boy left for college and she did not see him again for many years.

Father was finding it difficult to make his bones work. They creaked and moaned at the slightest provocation. The skin between his fingers was loosening, going rubbery. He was slipping away from himself. There were things out in the jungle he had seen but didn't quite believe. Shadows that shifted their shapes when he looked at them. Forms that danced at the edges of his vision. Once, when he was awakened in the night by the sound of heavy rain on his tent, he opened the flap and swore he saw pears falling from the sky.

One morning he spotted a rustling in the leaves at the edge of the fields. He crouched down low and sighted through his rifle the flashing black blur of a figure. He felt a nick in his heart and a charley horse in his chest. He waited for its next move and hoped it would not make one. Then it darted forward and he could make out the ruined tan of a man's face, a sneer worming over his lips. "Stop!" Father shouted. "In the name of the emperor!" There was a pause, and then the man moved nearer again, the green grass blades bending and waving to Father now like hands with broken fingers. "Stop at once!" he repeated, "or I'll shoot!" If the man heard him he did not seem to care.

When he ran to make sure the figure was dead, Father was horrified to turn the body over and find the face of the private. He buried him quickly, without ceremony, and washed his hands with canteen water until the container was empty. After returning to camp he was shocked anew: both men were there to greet him, intact and concrete. There were demons about this place, Father thought. He would have to be more careful.

Maemi decided to study genetics at Kyoto University. She spent many evenings in the lab, building rungs of DNA into a ladder of inheritance. Her hair still fell over her face and her eyes still strained to focus on others, but many men in the science department took an interest in her. During her first semester she lost her virginity to an entomology professor, pinned beneath him like one of his beetles. At the annual faculty party he introduced her to his wife. Maemi smiled as they shook hands, then locked herself in the coatroom and hit herself on the upper thigh until the tears retreated. There would be other men after him and each one would hurt a little bit less.

In her second year at school she got a phone call from Uncle. Her mother had not been feeling well the previous few weeks. When she went to see a doctor, they discovered cancer rooting in her stomach, spreading its poison limbs through her body. "She wants you to come home to see her, Mutton Chop," Uncle said. The line crackled between them. Anger writhed in Maemi like blood. How could her mother leave her? How much more grief must she gather? How much more family could she forge? "I don't know when I can get away," she said, unwept tears braiding in her throat.

At the funeral the next month Uncle wrapped two limp arms around her and told her she was welcome to stay with him whenever she liked. But without her mother there it didn't feel right. He had never been her father and he certainly couldn't be so now. During the holidays and summers she went to live with boyfriends instead.

The private and lieutenant were restless. They paced in their huts day and night. Voices swirled around but none belonged to the emperor. The jungle whispered secrets to itself. The stars snickered at them from above. "Why is there no word from him?" they asked. But their doubting only strengthened Father's resolve. Their mission was a sacred one and it required an obedience that not every man was capable of. He would stay until the end, no matter how it came.

But then the private wandered off and did not return. They waited until evening to search for him, the moon above casting a phantom glow over the trees. Each cracking branch beneath their feet was a premonition. Father held his breath like a glass he feared breaking.

They found the private on the outskirts of the forest, spread eagle and face down. His hair was matted. When Father touched the back of the private's neck, his fingers came away freckled with blood. The bullet, wherever it had come from, had killed him instantly. The lieutenant, when he saw the carnage, turned away and heaved up air. Father steeled his own stomach and rolled the private over. His face was unmarked; in the light his features had a guileless calm. "What have you done?" the leaves murmured. But what had they done? Who was this man, now dead twice over? They agreed to return for him the next morning, but when they came back the body was gone.

Three weeks before her twenty-fourth birthday Maemi married her last sweetheart. He was a stern but thoughtful man, an accomplished physics professor who spent hours locked up in his office, parsing through the riddles of the universe. She had loved men with their heads in the sky before, but never one with a purpose for being there. He was a man unlike any she had ever known, which allowed her to believe he could be like her father. He had recently been declared an official casualty of the old war.

They settled in Kawagoe, not far from her husband's school in Tokyo. He did not like her to work, so she had given up on her research, remaining at home to cook meals and otherwise wait out the day. Sometimes she went to Kitain Temple and walked among the hundreds of Gohyaku Rakan, the tiny statues of Buddhist disciples packed together like stone sardines, their faces sanded down from years of exposure so they all seemed to be sleeping. Sometimes she bent down to whisper secrets in their ears. She would be dutiful, she told them, and that would bring her closer to love.

Her husband handled her body like it was an equation, delicate and decipherable. Sometimes late in the night, after they had made love and her husband had gone to sleep, Maemi would lie awake and imagine the molecules of the world pinging around her, cells binding up and breaking apart, the living and the dead existing beside one another if only for a short while.

By the twenty-ninth year in the jungle Father was the only one who remained at the post. Not long after the death of the private, the lieutenant abandoned camp during the night. But Father's existence continued as it had before: scavenging for food, sleeping out beneath the stars, and awaiting word from the emperor. He did not consider himself lonely. It had been long enough for the isolation to simply become a life.

He allowed himself to dream again. He saw himself out one morning on the perimeter of the fields, performing his routine surveillance, when a figure approached him. It was a young man, shaggy haired and dressed in strange loose clothing, not more than thirty years old. He held his hands up, a reporter's camera strapped over his chest, and asked for his name. When Father gave it, the young man smiled and said, "I've been looking for you." He told him that the war had ended long ago. He pleaded with him to come home. But Father refused. "I am awaiting orders," he said.

The young man kept returning to him night after night, always saying the same thing. The war is over. We did not win. Finally he came with a delegate from the emperor's service. After Father was relieved of his duty and pardoned for any crimes committed while believing himself at war, he presented the delegate with his rifle. Then he dropped to his knees and wept until his body gave out beneath him. It was a dream so real and yet so curious, so filled with a foreign longing, it was as if someone else had given it to him.

Maemi did not remember her old childhood love right away when she answered the door. They had both grown older, of course, but it was more than that. His body was long and knobby as a green bean. His curiosity had hardened into philosophy. The child at her hip squirmed so at first Maemi did not hear what he was saying. Something about an island. Her father living there. He would be returning home soon. There would be a parade.

An island. Her father. Living. A shudder ran through her and though her body heaved with tears she did not shed them, not until later while her daughter was out playing in the backyard and she wept over the stove, salting the soup with her tears. That night, as her husband slept beside her, Maemi drifted off with a single image forming in her mind, the dream that all her other dreams had been guiding her toward: Father in an open-top car, sitting in the back with a representative of the emperor. He'd been given sunglasses and a new suit to wear, which itched at his elbows and knees. His hair had been cut back to the military cropping of his youth. Bits of gray peppered his chin hairs.

As they began the long drive down the avenue and the crowds of cheering people came into view on either side, he turned his head upward to the silver cyclopean buildings he still had not gotten used to living beneath. It was a strange world now, far stranger than the one he had left, and frightening too. So much noisier and faster and careless. And yet Father would face it all for what was waiting for him at the end of this journey: his daughter and grandchild. He would know them in an instant. He would take them both in his arms and tell them he was sorry that he had missed so much. He would kiss the tops of their foreheads, run his fingers through the soft strands of their hair. The approach was slow but it did not matter. For now he was content with the knowing that comes before being known.

Laika

Babette came to the home the same year we got a television. They arrived three days apart, both dropped unceremoniously at the front door. Madame Durance never bothered much with new girls but was very put out by the lack of paperwork for the strange machine. "We need to keep track of these things," she said, nudging the box with her sensible shoe. "What if it makes us all sick?" Hollis, the orderly, had it hooked up within an hour. It was 1957, the year Khrushchev looked up to a star-drunk sky and found a new world to conquer. We were all hankering for the unknown, though we knew that could be harder to find in Nebraska.

Babette, however, was left to dawdle in the hall, regarding her new surroundings with a ginger eye. She had a stooped posture that made her appear smaller than she was; the sack dress she wore was so thin it seemed in danger of dissolving with each new breath. Her hair fell in Grimm-like golden ringlets down her back, anointing her in a light that seemed both suspect and enviable. She could as easily have come from Hollywood as Omaha.

"Babette," Madame Durance repeated when she asked who she was. I could see her mulling it over, the name that sounded at once Biblical and lewd. "You'll bunk with her," she said, nodding toward me. All the new ones did.

It was an unspoken rule that the girls were not to ask each other what brought them to Durance Home. It was simple enough to guess some of their troubles, at least the ones with the bellies already in orbit, dropped off by the family priest. They'd grow big, disappear for a day or two, then return with bodies pressed flat like they'd been through a juicer. Nothing left but tears. The rest were dragged in by their mothers. I was brought by my brother, the only family I had; my slippery fingers had found their way into one pocket too many. He bought me a chocolate malt on the drive there—the last ice cream I would taste until adulthood. The woods around the home were filled with brocade trees. Deer flashed past like hoaxes. When we pulled up to the gate with its jack-o'-lantern teeth, it was blocked by ogling boys that Madame Durance shooed away. Like pigeons. When he left, my brother kissed my cheek, his whiskers leaving little cat scratches on my skin. That was 1954. I was ten. He died eleven years later in Vietnam; I remember the look on Madame's face when she told me, more clearly than anything about him. But Babette, far as anyone could tell, arrived alone.

Televisions were made of tubes in those days. There was enough time between turning the knob and the light snaking through its electric guts to wonder what exactly you were going to see. After Hollis finished plugging everything in, we all stood around the squat brown cube, observing its bulging poker face and insectile antenna. Nobody wanted to be the first to touch it. We had heard of them, certainly, but if anyone had been in the presence of one before, she didn't say so. "Step back," Madame Durance shouted, "I'm not paying for your medical bills if you all get cancer."

Then she leaned over and switched on the knob. The screen flickered, fuzzed, a low hum agitating the air. We waited silent, fingers in mouths, breath held. Madame Durance thwacked the side once and then the image caught, stilled. An old man, caterpillar-lipped, hair combed in white peaks, was seated at a desk, looking straight at us while he spoke. We all flinched in one great wave and then we started to listen. Someone named John Glenn had set a new transcontinental speed record, flying a supersonic jet from California to New York in three hours twenty-three minutes eight seconds. We all looked up as if he were still above us, as if we could see something other than the ceiling.

"Only one hour a day," Madame Durance said, fixing small padlocks over the knobs. But we could still be carried into sleep on visions of staticky life.

Later that year the Soviets launched two Sputniks into space. The first was just a satellite, a shiny metal sphere elbowing its way through the constellations. The second had a dog in it. Laika. Russian for "barker," the old man in the television said. A stray from the streets of Moscow. A blurry image of her in her flight harness was shown. The tips of her ears flopped down. The fur of her face was dark, kissed with ashes, except for one line of white that ran from her forehead down the length of her snout. Before she was shuffled into her own metal sphere, she turned back to the cameras and smiled like a starlet.

At night in our house on that little hill, when there were no lights for miles and the only sound was the breath in Babette's nose like the cooing of a dove, I would dream about Laika and what she saw up there. That sky so big it could swallow you. Keep you safe and warm.

Though Madame Durance did not pay much mind to how the girls arrived, she carried a different tune when it came to how they left. We were not prisoners, serving out a stay, but we were not quite wards either, kept confined until our eighteenth birthdays, when we were left to the whims of the world. We were there for our betterment, a betterment that was decided upon by Madame, and once betterment was reached, a mysterious transaction was performed and a parent or guardian showed up to take us home. This was a process we accepted rather than observed. One day a bed was empty, a girl was gone, and we were left believing that she had learned something but not knowing what it was.

By the time Babette arrived I had been in the home for three years and was losing interest in bolstering the sort of behaviors that would get me out. I was not, as my brother routinely reminded me, a pretty girl. My hair was the same color whether dirty or clean. I was solid as a tree trunk with the complexion of curdled milk. I wasn't made for much more than scrubbing floors, which was also my daily task at the home, lacking the parents to pay my keep. Still, Madame saw something in me. To this day I cannot name it. But a trust of sorts had formed between us. During my first few weeks at the home she would leave things out for me: a pencil case, a snow globe, a silvery thimble. A test to see if I would steal them away. Sometimes I did. But I grew to anticipate the tilted smile she gave me when I left something untouched. I began to recognize the glory in giving things away and became her confidante.

Most of the other girls were incessant talkers and boasters, having just recently recognized they were interesting, if only to one another, though they quickly learned to hold their tongues around me. Once they realized how their secrets reached the ears of Madame Durance, I was promptly snubbed. A room change was requested; another newcomer was installed. But I couldn't help myself. The rest of them chattered away to anyone within earshot, but Madame truly listened. It seemed the source of her power. I knew what to tell her, which seemed the source of mine.

Babette was a quiet girl and thus a figure of great curiosity for everyone else. She was peppered daily with questions, getting well-seasoned in a week.

"How did you get here?" they would ask. "By car?" "On foot?" "In a plane?"

She would dip her chin and smile in a way that suggested her pleasure couldn't be shared. "I was led here by the Lord," she'd say.

Every night before bed Babette knelt at the window and prayed. When I wanted to know why, she said it was because she was closer to God that way. "Does that mean your prayers get to him quicker?" I asked.

She laughed, a bright, trickling sound. It startled me in a way I never quite recovered from. "Come," she said, patting a spot on the floor beside her. "We'll see who He answers first."

I sat down, mimicking her pressed-hand pose, bending my forehead to my fingertips. But I had never asked God for anything but forgiveness, forced into the darkness of the confessional to recite my litany of petty crimes to a man I couldn't see. "You lie" was the only thing I had ever heard in return.

"I don't know what to do," I mumbled into the hollow between my thumbs.

"You don't have to do anything," Babette whispered. "Just let your thoughts wander where they need to go. He'll follow you."

I thought about Laika, looked up at the sky above us and the impossible cradle that carried her. I imagined her passing through the stars and being accepted as one of their own, each small bright ball leading her gently along her path. I thought of her smile flashing across the television screen, all the hope she held in her, and I wished her safely home.

The mystery of Babette's troubles revealed itself soon enough. About six weeks after she arrived, she started getting sick.

"Is she sitting too close to the television?" Madame Durance asked. But we all knew what it was.

Another week later Babette and I were called into her office. Madame Durance sat behind her desk, hands knitted in a neat fist. Her hair mirrored her hands: a high, tight bun coiled so close to her head it surely required pins to hold it, though I never saw any. She had the same stern look of that man on the television but she wanted to know the news rather than give it. "You've been here a month and a half," she began. "Do you want to tell me how long you've known?"

I watched Babette in the baldly nosy way that children are allowed to look at one another. She had a curious calm about her face that I'd never seen in the presence of Madame before. Most girls cowered, confessed before they were accused or fought back viciously. Babette simply sat there with the same serene, bemused expression of someone taking in an unusual entertainment. "I need to know when it happened, Babette."

She shook her head but the gesture was so small that it seemed she was neither refusing nor denying.

"I need to know if it happened here." Still, Babette remained silent.

Madame Durance turned to me. "Have you noticed anything . . . unusual happening recently? Somewhere on the grounds? Perhaps even in your room?"

I shook my head, knowing full well the long withering look that would follow. But what else could I do? It was the truth.

"Babette," she said, "who have you been having . . . intercourse with?"

"Nobody," she replied. Her voice was gentle but firm, the way a mother might cut off an argument with a troublesome child.

"I beg your pardon?" Madame's tone was cold enough to skate across.

"Any baby in me," she said, "was gifted by the Lord. Like Mary." Now it was Madame's turn for private amusement.

We were both dismissed, but Madame found me later in the third floor latrine, up to my elbows in soapsuds. "There's something off about that girl," she said. "I don't trust her. It happened here, I just know it. She needs looking after. And I need you to do it."

It was a test of a different sort, the first order Madame had ever given me and one that in the days after the revelation I found difficult to follow. There was no reason to believe Babette, of course, except that all of us did. "What's it feel like?" "What did you see?" "Did He speak to you?" One girl, Cordelia, affluent of breast and impoverished in brain, even asked for a lock of Babette's hair, as if holiness was something you carried on you, not in you.

Madame's skepticism seemed ugly in comparison, or at least unfair. She fired Hollis. She had to, she explained, to set an example for the other girls. It was a mistake to hire a man in the first place. Through it all Babette remained peaceful as a river, suggesting wild and wonderful things at work just underneath.

Every girl of that lost age has something she never quite got over. For some it was the first time they heard Bob Dylan. For others it was the sight of Paul Newman striding onscreen in *Hud*. For me it was Laika. Though there was little available at the time, in the years since I've been able to learn much about her. The Russians only had four weeks to build the spacecraft for her flight, for instance, but they made many provisions for her. There was an oxygen generator and a device to absorb carbon monoxide. An automatic fan was installed to keep the interior cool. Enough food was stored for a seven-day flight, and Laika was fitted with a bag to collect her waste. Monitors of all sorts kept track of her movements, her heart. She was estimated to be about three years old. Vladimir Yazdovsky called her "quiet and charming."

She was trained with two others, Albina and Mushka. To adapt the dogs to the confines of the craft's tiny cabin, they were kept in progressively smaller cages for periods of up to twenty days.

Such captivity caused them to stop urinating or defecating, made them twitchy and weak. The trainers tried giving them laxatives. But only by prolonging the internment could anything come of it. Later they were placed in centrifuges that simulated the movement and noises of the spacecraft during launch. Their pulses doubled; their blood pressure increased. They came out with the addled velocity of the elderly.

Before the launch, Dr. Yazdovsky took Laika home to play with his children. "I wanted to do something nice for her," he would later say. "She had so little time left to live."

Every once in a while, if it had been a long time since an incident, we were taken out into the world for a field trip. Madame Durance would rent a bus and those of us who were allowed to go piled in for the drive. Boys ran alongside, blowing kisses, leaving damp prints on the windows. This was the only touch of a boy I'd ever known: ghostly, quick to fade. I liked it that way.

The year Babette was with us we went to the town's art museum. It was a small, modest place whose walls were usually adorned with rolling hillsides and farmers forking hay. But that fall a painting was on loan from New York City, touring the country like a band or a play.

It stood alone on a far wall, a rope mounted around it to prevent anyone from getting too close. Most of the girls studied it for a minute or two before moving on, darting about in the unfamiliar space as if the full force of their locomotion could slow down time, could keep them there. But I was transfixed by what I saw: in the foreground a woman in a pink dress, dark hair in a low bun. She was sprawled out on an open field, her fingers gripping the half-dead grass. Her face was turned away, looking toward a gray house on the horizon, a place that I would never see her reach. Her name was Christina, so the plaque said. Though suffering from polio, she refused the use of a wheelchair. The artist was inspired to paint her after watching her crawl across a field from a window in his house.

It must have taken her hours. What sort of person could just stand by and observe something like that? But it was a hopelessness there's no helping. Like Laika. Like all of us, I suppose. Perhaps capturing it was all that could be done; it was, in its way, the only chance of honoring it.

The noise of the other girls brought me back, the tumble of their laughter, the scuff of their shoes on the floor. I blinked, glanced around, felt color creeping into my cheeks though nobody had taken any notice of my stupor. They burbled with hidden mirth, danced figure eights around one another. It dawned on me as I watched that Babette was not among them. She had disappeared.

Fear like hunger pangs filled me, doubled me over. Everywhere I looked were faces I knew but couldn't comprehend. My lungs twisted into strange balloon animal shapes. When Madame turned to reprimand a group of tittering girls, I slipped out the door and into the courtyard, gasping for new air.

Only one of us had ever tried to run before and she had come back: Cordelia, the girl who wanted to hold onto holiness. A friend posing as a brother had come to visit and smuggled her away. She was gone five days before her mother returned her, dragging her in by her hair as she kicked up a feral dust. "Goddammit, Cordie," her mother had cried, "why would you leave this?" She glanced at those of us who'd gathered, a wall of widening eyes. "This place is better than home." The bewildered look on her face as she said this is one I've never forgotten. But I knew Madame's response to my failure would be even more enduring.

Once my breath caught up with me, another sound made itself known. It was Babette, her hands making tiny arcs across her stomach, sitting on a bench beneath the bosom of a wilting tree.

From a distance she appeared to be shivering, but as I drew closer I heard the lamb bleats of her distress. "It hurt," she said as I sat beside her.

"Are you okay?" I asked, looking her over for cuts and bruises, thinking one of the girls had done something to her. "Do you want me to get Madame?"

Her head gave a violent shake. "When it happened. It hurt. Why didn't He tell me?" she said. "What if He made a mistake choosing me?"

As startling as it can be to hear such doubt from an adult, I've come to believe over the years that it's more frightening when it comes from a child. It seemed it was my duty to comfort her in that moment. Perhaps even my destiny.

"No," I said, less because I believed it than I wanted her to, "God doesn't do that."

She took a deep breath, wiped at her tears, and when I looked at her again there was a calmness in her eyes that dwarfed her age.

"You sure you're okay?" I asked.

Babette just smiled in that internal way she had. The way that said she trusted herself more than the world. Just like adults did.

Laika died on the fourth day of the flight. Though she succeeded in her mission, her machine failed her. The Block A core of the satellite didn't detach as planned. She overheated in orbit after the thermal insulation tore loose, raising the temperature in the cabin to over 100 degrees.

The Soviets had always planned for her death. They had hoped to euthanize her; her seventh serving of food was poisoned. For forty-five years the scientists offered conflicting reports on the mission, a deception that allowed the Russian, and eventually the American, programs to continue their march toward successful human spaceflight. Laika's true demise was not revealed until

October 2002, when one of the scientists presented a paper at the World Space Congress in Houston, Texas. "It turned out that it was practically impossible to create a reliable temperature control system in such limited time constraints," he said in the newsclip.

About five months after the launch, on April 14, 1958, Sputnik 2 disintegrated upon reentry into the Earth's atmosphere, carrying Laika's remains with it. By then everyone else had moved on. Other, greater missions lay ahead.

A few months passed. There was a cold spell and a new year. We grew older, grew bigger, some of us grew less bad and left.

Then on a Tuesday in February Babette's brother, Luther, came to visit her. She didn't seem surprised to see him, but then again she hadn't seemed surprised by anything as long as we'd known her. Though Madame Durance eyed him over suspiciously, his Beat poet hair and mud-lashed pants, she let him in. I was put in charge of watching them.

Though Madame usually sat right at the table with visitors, I chose a seat a bit more removed. This was part politeness and part curiosity; I wanted to have a good view of any cracks in Babette's manner. Though she did not meet the hand her brother offered her, she treated him with the same dreamy courtesy as anyone else I'd seen her with in the home. He seemed pained by this or perhaps by everything, wincing without warning, as if from countless invisible blows.

"Nice place here," he said. She nodded, waited, resting her arms on her belly like it was a windowsill. How strange to watch families interact this way, as if a new place also made them new to each other.

"You're big," he said.

"Yes," she smiled. "The Lord has blessed me."

Sourness passed over his face. "Too late, then," he said.

"The Lord has blessed you too."

"I don't want it."

"You can't talk like that."

"You don't want it neither," he said. "I know."

I didn't feel so good then, like my whole body was caught in a shiver that wouldn't stop. It was how he was looking at her. Like she was the bone his teeth kept gnawing.

"All babies are blessings," she said.

"You got the devil in you."

She took his hand, pressed it first to her lips and then to her stomach. He jumped like lightning. When he pulled it back, held it up as if to hit her, she was never anything but calm. Graceful, even. "I forgive you," she said.

When I told Madame what I had heard, she looked at me with the narrowed eyes of a skeptic. "Her own brother?" she scoffed. "Why would you say something like that?" It seemed there were limits to the badness even Madame would believe.

"Madame," I said, panic and protest rising in me at once, clouding my eyes with tears. I let them spill over recklessly; she hated this sort of blubbering even more than lies.

"You should know better," she said. "Perhaps Durance Home has done what it can for you. There are other places girls like you can be." Then she went back to the papers on her desk, not even bothering to dismiss me.

These words came back to me later that night when I heard our bedroom door click open, the soft rustle of someone wanting not to be heard, and then a cry muffled by a swift clamping motion. I felt a curl of sickness in my stomach, sweat flocking in my pits, my heart slashing me like a razor. I stayed still, kept my breathing steady, even when she bit his hand and grunted out something. The start of my name soon snuffed. I knew the places Madame spoke of. My brother and I had been shuffled in and out of them for years before Durance Home, whenever another relative got tired of us. So I shrank from the sounds of their struggle, the violence I didn't want turned on me, until the door shut behind them, leaving me alone in the smothering silence.

As the terror of the moment began to subside, another stranger feeling began to build in me: relief. I would be blamed for it, I knew, but what I said would be believed. She was just another runaway now. I would be safe.

Fifty years after her remains returned from space, Laika was memorialized in a statue and plaque, unveiled on April 11, 2008, in Star City, Russia, not far from the military facility where she was trained. It depicts a dog standing on top of a rocket. Though few in Russia spoke out about the controversy of the mission before the fall of the regime, Oleg Gazenko, one of the scientists who worked with Laika, has since said, "The more time passes, the more I'm sorry about it. We shouldn't have done it . . . We did not learn enough from this mission to justify the death of the dog."

Over the years I have thought about Laika often, and Babette too, turning them over in my mind like a Rubik's cube that never quite clicks into place. Laika's story is known though not well recorded, which is its own kind of tragedy. I have wondered what became of Babette, if there was any joy in the life she was dragged back to. Even now some nights I dream her and Luther into the bed beside me, limbs writhing together like a den of snakes, my name like venom on her tongue. I wake up screaming loud enough to be heard, not just in other rooms but in other years.

A girl appeared here, not too many months ago, with the same blonde hair, the same inward smile. A granddaughter perhaps? No. She was no child of God, that one.

I've been at Durance Home for close to sixty years now, taking care of it myself for thirty, though I have never thought to change the name. The girls call me "Miss" anyway. I know what they think. Behind my back it's "Sister." In a way the slur makes sense; I'm performing a penance of sorts.

I haven't left the grounds since Madame died. Even before that I rarely wandered very far. It took time to rebuild Madame's trust, but we both knew I didn't belong anywhere else. I didn't have the schooling for college or the manners for a husband. A shame it's not like it used to be. I understand the cruelty of the young better than most. But there's no respect, no fear, in these girls now. They tussle with one another, cuss and scream. They see nothing worth learning in my lessons. I'm ruining their lives keeping them here, not keeping them from ruining themselves. I want them safe; they wish me dead. The woods around us have grown scalp bald but sometimes they still disappear into them. And it just gets worse with time. There is no one to continue this work after me, but I'm getting on in years. That's what makes me saddest of all. I'm not so eager to return to the world when this is all I see of it.

Perhaps I have been wrong to think of Laika's death as a tragedy. After all, if she had been able to return, what kind of life would she be coming back to? A hero's welcome, surely, but then? A family to take her in? To eke out her remaining years manhandled by some ignorant child, dreaming of another orbit? There was no sorrow in being chosen in the first place, saved from a street-wandering squalor, to be fed and if not loved, then trusted. Some of us are meant to bear the glory that the rest of us merely share in. At least Laika was allowed that moment of awe, when the stars were surrounding her, and the moon, still so far from reach, was looking at her funny, wondering what she was doing there.

Foreigners

Rebecca noticed the lights first. A blue then a red pirouetting on the edge of her page as she turned it. She was reading in the front parlor after dinner, seated by the picture window that was designed to set scenes like this: her neighbor, Anya Demidov, being led by the police from the driveway she'd just pulled into, a bag of groceries still cradled in her arms.

There was one cop on either side of her, each gripping an elbow, steering her to a silvered crosshatch of cars parked in front of her house. As she walked, her ponytail swung back and forth with the judgment of a wagging finger. She knew her audience, kept her neck straight, her head high as if she was in etiquette class instead of handcuffs. Later, Rebecca would remember that there were no sirens. In the moment, as she watched Anya's face toughen and shrink, her features fired in a kiln of her own devising, she was just one part of a silence so full and complete it was as if it was waiting to be heard.

The others watched from their windows or from behind their front doors, more felt than seen, the neighborhood holding its collective breath as the trio approached the squad car. When Anya was pivoted into position, the bag she'd been holding split in two. Tin cans and produce tumbled to the street.

The three of them stood there, heads bowed in silent communion. When Anya bent to gather the twirling tops of her groceries, the officers yanked her back up in a motion of such efficient violence that it sucked the air right out of Rebecca's rigid body. Anya's head was lowered and her form was accepted into the groping darkness of the backseat. Then they pushed off into the night as if none of it had happened, leaving the porch lights on behind them. At some point, after everyone had exhausted themselves with speculation and laid down for a fitful sleep, a timer turned them off.

"What's so special about the Demidovs?" Colin asked. Rebecca looked across the dinner table at her son and resisted the urge to flick the hair that brazenly dangled in his eyes, the same hair she used to place a bowl on to cut and that she hadn't touched without consequences in years. Yet again he had sculpted the components of his meal into artful piles rather than eating them. If his father had been there he'd have made him lick up every last lump. But his father wasn't there, and besides, the counselor had told Rebecca to be more accommodating to her son's needs. "Nothing," she said. Then, "Why do you ask?"

It had been a few days since the arrest but the novelty had kept it current and likely would remain so for months. Rebecca had been living in the town for longer than the marriage that first brought her there, though she felt, like everyone, as if she'd been there forever. When they'd first moved in, her husband spoke expansively of setting down their roots. But instead the neighborhood had hardened into a carapace around them, trapping her in a town where every teen pregnancy and illicit affair was more sport than secret.

"I ask because they're on fucking CNN."

Colin had long stopped responding when she objected to his language, though Rebecca half-heartedly continued with the charade. But the images flashing on the muted television caught her eye first: Anya accepting a plaque from the mayor, her hair done up in a challah braid, her smile a spray of teeth. The husband, who everyone called Mick. A professor of Eastern European studies with a bulldog's body. Single women in the neighborhood were always sending him up ladders or under sinks. A portrait of their daughter, Zora, with her bottle-bottom glasses and visor of bangs, the stick of her body bent over the keys of a grand piano. A quiet, introspective child two grades behind Colin in school but enrolled in several of his classes. He complained of her often but what would become of her now?

Rebecca plucked a few words from the sprinting ticker tape on the bottom of the screen: Infiltration, Allegation, Deportation. Spies. Such an old-fashioned word now. Quaint, even. Was she just imagining the sadness in their faces? Or had the possibility of this day always been upon them, pressing the ends of their mouths slightly downward?

Then, with a shock, it was their house on display, at once alien and iconic, like seeing the Eiffel Tower for the first time after years of travel shows. A woman in a charcoal pantsuit was standing at the Demidovs' front door, leading the camera around the perimeter, her hands making gestures of mysterious portent. The curtains were all drawn, though that had always been the case. When Colin was younger he used to call it the house that never woke up.

They'd been neighbors for nine years but Rebecca had never stepped beyond their front door. When the Demidovs moved in, she brought over a casserole. A few days later Anya returned the dish, filled with a dinner of her own. Their relationship since, like many of imposed proximity, was one of clockwork politeness and veiled antagonism. They waved, honked their horns, admired one another's landscaping. But the Demidovs didn't live in the neighborhood so much as adorn it with their presence. They installed a pool in their backyard and regularly hosted outdoor parties in the summers. Rebecca and her husband were often invited but always declined, at his insistence. "Becky," he'd complain, using the old nickname he knew irritated her, "I got married so I wouldn't have to go to shit like that anymore." Then they'd sit on the couch watching television and not speaking to one another. Peeking through her windows at the tiki torches, teased by the strums of a ukulele, Rebecca would feel like a loiterer in her own home.

"You think they did it?" Colin asked.

Anya had only come into her house once, not long after Rebecca's husband moved out. In the days after the U-Haul truck pulled half her life away, she had been subjected to looks of withering pity and robotic condolences. So when Anya showed up at her door with a bottle of vodka, she let her in as much out of necessity as gratefulness, an urge to bludgeon her mind from her body.

Though the bounce of Anya's name belied a grave disposition, she made an amiable drinking companion, or at least one content to let Rebecca's garbled monologues run their course. They sat at the kitchen table and traded shots that cauterized her gums and turned her tears septic. Late in the evening, when Rebecca's peripheral vision had frayed and her tongue could no longer keep up with her thoughts, Anya confessed that she had thought more than once of leaving Mick. "But I cannot," she said in a voice that sounded suspiciously unspoiled by drink. "We are too much tethered." When Rebecca pressed her on the point, Anya quickly withdrew. In the five years since, neither had mentioned the night again. They were both better performers than that.

"Yes," Rebecca said, wiggling her fork into her mound of mashed potatoes. "Yes, I think they did it."

Around town people were just as often identified by the characteristics of their houses as by their names. There was the couple rumored to be sleeping in separate beds; everyone called their place the "split level." There was the local postman who kept several pickups, all grizzled with rust and parked along the street, which was openly referred to as the "cul-de-sac-of-shit." On gracious days Rebecca lived in the "ivory tower." On others she was the "uppity bitch with the turret."

The Demidovs lived in a nondescript house, blue with white shutters, boldly ordinary in hindsight. They were referred to simply as "the foreigners." The nickname wasn't meant to chafe. For many in the neighborhood the presence of such educated, adaptable immigrants was a source of pride. They were prepackaged exotic, unthreatening but still interesting, and they had a way of seeming curious about anyone they came across, a talent that now seemed deflective if not outright suspect. Everyone wanted to be liked by them. Now everyone was claiming they'd been on to them.

Rebecca spent her afternoons at home, earning a negligible income by teaching piano lessons to neighborhood children. She stood behind them while they played, though very rarely did they achieve the fluidity to reach that description. Instead they banged on the keys like they were driving a square peg into a round hole. But she didn't lament her pupils' carelessness or brutality. None of them were being groomed; merely distracted for an hour.

In the beginning she had made an effort to impart her limited wisdom to her students. Zora Demidov had been one of her first, though she showed little interest in the Mussorgsky Rebecca hoisted on her, preferring the plinking goosesteps of Satie. She had the sort of stiffness that might one day mellow into grace. But her talent quickly outgrew Rebecca's capacities and she was shuffled off to a private tutor after only a month. Rebecca hadn't had a student with her promise since, and these days she found her eyes wandering to the windows while the students played, her mind a spinning top.

That's why, a week after the arrest, she was the first to notice the car, a little black hump blocking the Demidovs' driveway. That day saw the first autumn downpour, the pellets hurtling toward the earth, punching lace into the leaves, bursting on the ground in fat plops. Plastic police crossing tape snapped in the wind. Whoever was sitting inside the car wouldn't come out. When Rebecca's last student left, she lingered on the stoop, smoking a cigarette tucked in the tines of a plastic fork. It was a method she'd picked up to hide the habit from her mother and she had never discarded it. Not even after moving above the Mason-Dixon line, twenty hours away from her. The wipers slashed across the windshield but the face remained a pointillist mystery. After a few minutes of enduring Rebecca's scrutiny, the car revved to life and drove off.

"You look a little spooky, Mom," Colin said at dinner that evening. He wore a black sweatshirt, zipped up to his Adam's apple, hood raised, his features shrinking into its shadows; Rebecca didn't think he looked particularly inviting himself. Then again, the person who greeted her in the mirror that morning had skin that was plowed-over pale, a stare as blank as quarters over the eyes of the dead. If by forty everyone has the face they deserve, Rebecca wanted a word with whoever was passing the judgments.

"Do I?" she said. "Been talking to ghosts I guess."

"Did Dad call?"

"No," she said instinctively. It'd been a long while since Rebecca had picked up the phone to hear her ex-husband saying her name. Every time he did it was like a bandage being ripped off. Not a new hurt so much as a reminder that one had existed once.

She often wondered if Colin missed his father. She'd been given sole custody, though she hadn't asked for it. The only stipulation at all had been over the child support. He'd pay it only if she remained in town. "I don't want you uprooting Colin now," he'd said. But she knew the truth. He was punishing her, snaring her in a place he'd prevented her from understanding with a child she'd long ago lost while he moved in with his secretary in the city, a two-hour drive away.

"How was school?" she asked, her favored remedy for lapses in conversation; she did it even in the summer.

"I didn't go."

"What?"

"Just checking," Colin smirked. "What's going on outside?"

"Nothing," Rebecca said. From her seat at the table she could see through the parlor to the front window. That evening, the lights of passing cars had worked their way into her circuitry; even when she wasn't looking she knew when they were coming. But the one she was hoping for hadn't reappeared.

"I'm sorry," she said. "How was school?"

"Our history professor told us about Stalin sending prisoners to Siberia," Colin said. "Do you think that's where Zora's parents will go?"

"Stalin doesn't send anyone anywhere anymore," Rebecca said, pausing to blow billowing steam from her spoon. "What did Zora have to say about it?"

"Nothing. She hasn't been in class since they got locked up."

"Oh, right. Of course." An image of Zora flashed through her mind, a tiny figure at a piano in a snowy field, her mittens dancing clumsily over the keys. "Anything else I should know?"

"I think I'm joining the Army."

Rebecca laughed, a dry sound that discouraged merriment rather than inviting it. Her ex-husband once described it as an axe splitting wood. "Timber," he used to yell in its wake.

Her son had often told her of the myriad ways he might leave her. Rarely did it involve college, which was what she wanted him to do. Again, her mind returned to Zora, to the parents who bore her. Of all the reasons to have offspring, companionship was a poor one. But wasn't doing it for appearance's sake worse? And yet the Demidovs had raised the better child.

"Can you even join the Army?" she asked. "Don't you have a record now?"

"There's no record if you're a witness."

A few weeks after the school year started, one of Colin's friends had been arrested for taking a shit on the porch of Eusapia Kessler, an elderly woman who used a walker and lived across the street from them. When Rebecca picked Colin up from the juvenile facility, he seemed remorseful. But since then the incident had become a sticking point between them.

"And what about Cami French?" Rebecca asked.

"She's not pressing charges," Colin said as soup drooled from his spoon. "Neither is Camp Friendship."

"Let's thank God for that."

"I don't thank God for anything."

"Well, He only forgives so many times."

Colin pushed his chair back from the table. The felt discs attached to its feet made the movement fluid rather than forced. Then he set his dishes in the sink and stalked out the front door.

These dinners had become the worst kind of compulsion, one performed in the service of some greater good that neither of them could clearly define anymore. It was no comfort knowing that every family surrounding them was enacting their own version of the same charade. There was not much to envy about the Demidovs now, but they had found a way to escape that fate.

One night not long after her husband had moved out, Rebecca had gotten into her car and driven off while Colin was sleeping. She'd gotten as far as the exit for the turnpike, could almost make out ahead of her the shimmering industrial obesity of the city before turning back, compelled less by a duty she truly felt than one she was merely aware of. Besides, there was nowhere else for her to go; the person she had been before no longer existed, the places she had lived long since remolded by time. Still, more than once she had wondered what would have happened to the Rebeccas who continued on, what life they would be leading now, all the things they had felt and seen that she wasn't brave enough to know. Now it was Colin who snuck out after dark.

Rebecca didn't enjoy grocery shopping. She was always running into someone with an opinion and the contents of her cart too clearly crystallized the person she'd become: one who valued convenience over care, a maternal delinquent. She moved about with the metallic clank of a factory, her soup cans and macaroni boxes jumping in unison as she raced over the tile, hemmed in on all sides by baskets filled with bristling fists of broccoli, pallets of grapefruits and lemons that pulsed in the corner of her eye.

On the way home she remembered: she'd neglected to get any groceries for Mrs. Kessler. It was a penance she'd taken on herself after what had happened, and Eusapia had wordlessly accepted it. But the store had set Rebecca on edge. In the driveway, with her car idling, she stuffed some of her purchases into a paper bag—potato chips, peanuts, frozen dinners, a bachelor's sustenance instead of a meal. A preemptive shame crept up her cheeks as she made her way to the house, well kept by those Eusapia paid to care for it. Behind her back, people called her property "the Crypt."

Eusapia answered the door and stepped out onto the porch, one gimpy wheel on her walker making her path wobbly. Though the old woman was cagey with everyone, Rebecca suspected a more barbed wariness was reserved for her and, fearing puncture, she moved around Eusapia in a way that could easily be mistaken for disgust. Being around her always reminded Rebecca that it'd been too long since she'd called her mother. Then she was reminded that her mother was dead.

"Hello, Rebecca," Eusapia said, hurrying the words out of her mouth. Up close she had the sort of slack skin that looked ready to be picked up and stretched over somebody new. Her clothes stunk of shredded newspaper.

"Hello, Mrs. Kessler," Rebecca replied. "You're looking well."

"I can't see your teeth, Rebecca. I'll have to assume you're lying through them. Put that down, I'll take it in."

Rebecca was already setting the bag on the ledge of the porch, well versed in the nuances of this farce, anticipating them in a way Eusapia might have found insulting if she cared. "You're sure?" Rebecca asked, glancing upward.

"Sure I'm sure," Eusapia said. "I've half a mind to ask you to stop this nonsense and let me shop for myself!" She became very interested in something on her collar, brushing and fluffing it for so long that Rebecca wondered if she should just turn away when Eusapia said, "Where's that Demidoff woman gone anyway?"

"I think she's gone home," Rebecca said.

"Home? Nonsense. I've seen that car parked out front. Nobody's there."

"Home country, I meant. You've noticed the car too?"

"Of course," Eusapia said. "It was trying so hard not to be seen I couldn't miss it."

"It's funny, right?"

They both inclined their heads slightly toward the yard across the street, neither wanting to be the one to turn in full. The car wasn't there but someone had taped a small American flag to a stick and planted it on the edge of the lawn.

"They were a strange lot, when you really think about it," Eusapia said. "Remember how they turned little Nicki Seltzin away when she was selling Girl Scout cookies? Telling a six-year-old that they don't support clubs that traffic commodities? I guess it's not that surprising someone's come sniffing around."

"I wonder who it could be," Rebecca murmured. "Another spy?"

Eusapia scoffed. "Don't be ridiculous. You can't spy on nobody. And they might as well be nobody now."

With that she turned back into her house and shut the door in Rebecca's face, leaving the bag of groceries behind on the ledge untouched. It was still there when she went out for a cigarette the next morning.

But Rebecca took little notice: the black car was in front of the Demidovs' drive again. She watched as a woman emerged, dressed in a gray suit, her hair pulled into a tight, business-like bun. She took something from the trunk, a sign that she then began hammering into the front lawn. Coldwell Banker, it proclaimed in bright screaming bold. House for Sale. A few moments later the woman went inside and began pinning back the curtains. Rebecca slipped back inside, feeling foolish and dismayed.

Not long after that the news well on the Demidovs began to dry up. The rest of the world, it seemed, was moving at a faster clip; there were catastrophic weather events to follow, diplomatic blunders to attend to. Even around the neighborhood people had found other things to talk about: a teacher's alleged transgression with a student, the city council's decision to remove a crucial stoplight downtown. Rebecca could feel herself growing more irrelevant every time she opened her mouth. What would be done with their furniture, their clothes? What about Zora's things? Surely there were precious items she'd left behind, items whose significance no one else could possibly understand. And who would come to take their place? "I'm goddamn tired of talking about this," Colin growled at the dinner table. But she couldn't stop bringing them up.

Finally she resorted to the synthetic clutches of the Internet, a world of gossips in invisibility cloaks. Rebecca scoured news sites and message boards for any mention of the family, but they were filled with nothing but empty speculation and petty arguments, confirming little more than the worst she'd already imagined. She was about to give up when she discovered a link to a video, described as a "Demidov Performance."

Rebecca clicked, watched the spinning white lines as it loaded, and was surprised to be greeted by a grand piano on the screen. Surprised, at least, until Zora entered, or a digitally diminutive version of her. She gave a somber bow to her unseen audience, then sat on the bench. She wore a strap to secure her glasses and Rebecca smiled in anticipatory recognition: when Zora played, she threw her head back in a sort of supplemental ecstasy, shaking it like an epileptic when a section required particular emphasis. The gesture didn't seem to come from joy so much as hunger, a need to fit her form into something much bigger than herself. Rebecca couldn't take her eyes off her. She was about to restart the video for the third time when the doorbell interrupted.

The police were on her stoop. Their uniforms fit in all the wrong places. One was a short busty black woman, the other a white man whose arms were wreathed in tattoos. What did the kids call that these days? Both of them held Colin up by his elbows. He had the air of someone wanting to be seen, his stringy arms straining with the effort to puff up his chest. "Ma'am," said the policeman, "is this your son?"

"I suppose it is," she replied. Sleeves. They called them sleeves. "Whose house did he desecrate this time?"

"So he's done this before?"

"That depends. Was he the one shitting on the porch or was it one of his friends again?"

"Ms. Speers," the policewoman said, her drawl a potent mix of sullenness and apathy, "your son broke into the house next door. He's being charged with destruction of property and resisting arrest."

One of Rebecca's nails dug a divot in her finger. "You mean the Demidovs'?" she asked.

"I mean the one that's vacant."

"But you're not arresting him?"

"Only room for four in the cell," the policewoman said, as her partner began unlocking the cuffs. "Someone'll be by tomorrow. Then he can take a turn all by his lonesome."

Rebecca looked at Colin's face for the first time and was startled to find victory on it. Not the victory of a child, full of glee and discovery, handling its newfound power like something easily broken. It was the taunting smirk of someone who had won the petty argument, was storing up ammunition for another stalemate. She was startled to recognize so clearly the old cruelties of a husband in a son, to realize just what they might have borne, and it reawakened an amniotic anger in her, one she hadn't felt for many years, one she had almost forgotten feeling at all. Then he spoke: "Sorry, Becky." She reached out and yanked him inside the house by his scruff.

The howl he let loose was a violent, thrashing thing; it must have followed the police all the way to their car. "What's wrong with you?" he asked quietly after Rebecca closed the front door behind them. He had aged years in a moment, the infantile agony of seconds before replaced by a concern almost comic in its gravity, like a child drowning in the folds of his father's suit. But something dark behind his eyes kept Rebecca from laughing.

"Colin," she said, careful to tailor her words to his tone. "What on earth were you thinking, going in there?"

"Maybe I thought I would do something unforgiveable," he said, his voice remaining as lethally measured as it had been before.

"What does that mean? Did you take something from the house?" Rebecca asked, not knowing if the possibility appalled or excited her. She pictured some small family memento, some piece of government secrecy, rubbing shoulders with his sweatshirt pocket, aching to be detected. Or maybe it was something he slipped into a sleeve in his wallet, sandwiched between a driver's license and an expired condom, still swaddled in its wrapping.

"Let me ask you something," he said. "Do you think you live in this house?" He swept his arm across himself instead of the room. Rebecca flinched and then blushed, knowing she had just given something of herself away.

"Of course I–

"No," he interrupted. "You stay here. That's not the same thing. Do you have any idea what people say about you?"

Of course she did. They said she was frigid, self-isolating, a snob, a rube. That she brought everything on herself. That she was by turns weak and spineless or had frightened off a good man. She knew all of these things. But she didn't know her son did, much less that he seemed to agree.

"Colin. Go upstairs." Her voice was so meek it frightened her to hear it.

"You can't keep me here, Mom. You don't keep anything. You see these walls, these shelves? They used to have things on them. Do you remember that?"

"Do you?"

Rebecca remembered very well the day, in the wake of her abandonment, she took the family photographs down from the walls and then, frames and all, stuffed them in black garbage bags along with his paperbacks with the shaggy spines, his gym shirts with the sandpapery pits, and took them to the city dump. She could recall looking over the hillocks of eviscerated furniture and cremated clothing and feeling as though she were part of some collective exhibition of feminine revenge. She remembered the blankness of the house afterward, that sense of purity, of possibility, that she'd lost almost as soon as she'd recognized it, replaced by the sudden oddness of her habits, still washing her hands in the sink, still stripping the sheets every week in a house with one less person in it. But how could Colin remember those things, or remember enough to believe he was a part of them? He'd been a child then, hadn't he?

"I'm going," he said, shrugging further into his sweatshirt before pushing past her. "I'll be back before anyone comes tomorrow. Don't worry about that. I can do my time."

"Okay," was all Rebecca could muster for the front door's clanging backside.

She must have gotten over there somehow, though she wouldn't remember what mechanics led her movements, even much later. She was first aware of the sizzling sound of crickets as she ducked past the police barrier and glided up the path to the front door, which someone had divested of its knob.

Inside the house had the air of a ransacked mausoleum; a ruptured heaviness lay over the toppled furniture and scattered curios, still throbbing like an open wound. It made her tread delicately through the rooms, as if a further disturbance would rob the wreckage of its meaning. The soft buzz of silence tickled her ears. It was strange to enter a place she'd so often imagined and find it in ruins; she felt she was imagining it still.

The layout was not unlike her own home and she wandered toward the back and into the kitchen. Outside, past the sliding glass doors, she could make out the slurry ripples of the pool, its surface now a carpet of foliage. The tiki torches had been bundled together like driftwood and left to lean against the fence, awaiting a party that would never resume. It was her first sense of truly trespassing, not on a place so much as on a moment in time. Her reverence was quickly conquered by her curiosity; she turned away from the window eager to see more.

Pots and pans were strewn about the kitchen floor, but the place-
mats on the dinner table had been left untouched, as had the silver-
ware, lined up on napkins that had been folded into triangles. The
fridge released a sour honey stench when she opened it; she leaned
in to inspect the fur-coated fruit and shriveled vegetables inside.
Someone had stuck a Post-It on the milk carton; its end curled up
at her, beckoning like a finger. Even though the note was written in
the inscrutable building blocks of Cyrillic, she pocketed it anyway.

In the wake of the fridge's fluorescence, the rest of the house
seemed mordantly dark. She drifted into the front parlor and pulled
the little brass cord on a Tiffany desk lamp, trapping her surroundings in amber light. She could see Eusapia's house across the street,
its brightness spilling all the way to the empty sidewalk. How long
had the old woman stood at the window and watched what the
boys were doing? There wasn't much in the room that hadn't had
a good going over. The stuffing had been pulled loose from the
couch cushions, puffing up like smoke from a plaid chimney. Entire
books had been de-spined, their pages laid out nakedly on the floor.
Rebecca shivered at the sight of some derogatory slang scratched
into the walls. It was the city dump domesticated, but there was
nothing redemptive in this disarray. Whatever secret shame the
Demidovs had been harboring had now transferred to her and she
would have left immediately if she hadn't noticed Zora's backpack.

It was slumped against the legs of a desk and seemed not to
have drawn the boys' notice. Until Rebecca opened it and found
Zora's math homework, the equations now resolved into cartoons
of genitalia. She dug deeper, past the stapled piano scores and
school supplies, as if the backpack held something essential to
Zora's being, the catalyst for the hunger she held inside herself
were Rebecca to only look hard enough.

When she reached the very bottom, all she found was a brightly
colored figurine shaped like a galloping horse. It stood no taller

than her hand; when she picked it up she was surprised by its lightness. As she ran her fingernail over the surface, its skin flaked away like soap. She had seen this sort of thing before, years and years ago, in the old notions shops her mother frequented down south. Normally her memories came to her dyed in iodine, like old photographs. But suddenly her childhood was before her in vivid Technicolor. She remembered the bleached white of the store's counters, the sly cat-eye pattern of the buttons her mother bought, the dark green of the Skee-Ball prize tickets that she hoarded to trade for trinkets. Her mother appropriated any tickets that went unused, a circumstance she only became aware of when a neighborhood girl tore open her teddy bear and a strange spinach stuffing emerged from his guts. When Rebecca mentioned this incident at a PTA meeting years later, the other women had given her wrinkled-nose looks, as if she were speaking another language.

Zora would remember this place, this neighborhood, whether or not she ever considered it a home, but what would she actually think of it? As she grew older, would she look back with fondness, if she looked back at all? Would she feel like Rebecca felt now, as if she'd been mugged by the passage of time? She had been so careful to shed every skin of her past but what did she have to show for it? How could they, everyone said, when the Demidovs were found out. But how could any of them? Surely someone in the neighborhood could remind them all of the things they'd given up, of the people they could have been. Perhaps it could be her. She was the only outsider left now. Was that footsteps she heard at the door just then? She would invite them all, she thought. She would invite them all in.

No Man's Land

Later, after I'd had a few years to get used to the idea, I wouldn't think of that summer as the one when my parents started sleeping in separate beds. I would think of the twenty-seven days of cold rain in June and how once my sister Addie and I ate popsicles while wearing mittens. I would think of the rap-rap-rap of the choir conductor's baton and the clear roving eye of the Ouija board planchette. Mostly, though, I would think of Ms. Flox, our brief and bewildering caretaker, who smoked cigarettes at windowsills and knew things about the world.

It was the first and only summer of Desert Storm and my father had recently been made a senior drill sergeant at Fort Dix in New Jersey. We moved into a complex just outside the base, set up for "Families of the Army" and composed of slapdash regulation houses that were issued a tri-fold flag. The unmarried soldiers called it "No Man's Land." We woke up to a recording of a bugle calling Reveille and kneeled down to pray to Taps.

In those early days, before school allowed us to define ourselves in our own terms, Addie and I became known as the "marching girls" for the way our father ran formations with us every morning. Left-left-left-right-left we'd clomp about the lawn in our nighties, thin will-o'-the-wisps that threatened to fly away at any moment, distracted by a butterfly or a bike with streamers. We were disappointing cadets and he had little hope for us.

Though anticipation of war had sharpened the air, making the adults move around more carefully, all I cared about was making friends. The children in the neighborhood were reckless and terrifying. They called me "Loose-End-Up" instead of Lucinda, an insult I didn't quite understand but that hurt just from the snarly way they said it. One boy, whose legs were cross-hatched with pink poison ivy scars, told us with ravenous glee about the wounds his father had sustained in Vietnam. "The blood kept coming from his stomach," he said, demonstrating with accompanying motions. He looked like a magician pulling a scarf from his coat.

Eventually, our mother tired of "picking our skulking faces off the floor" and we were enlisted in the Fort Dix Children's Choir. On the second Tuesday of June, dressed in white tights turned transparent by the rain, we shuffled into the chapel with a group of children varying in size and level of enthusiasm. The chapel was a small building at the edge of the base, made from the same mold as the barracks that stood beside it. In the coming months it would hold three weddings, one baptism, and a funeral, but all I knew of it then was that it had the atmosphere of an armpit.

The man behind the upright piano had a face like a full moon, pale and bright and cheesy. His name was Mr. Giletti, and by way of greeting he rapped his baton on the wood and cried, "Boys here. Girls there." We parted. "Now show me your lungs!"

"Oh, my little Maria Callases," our mother said, when we returned home.

"Show me what you've learned," said our father.

The notes hit some snags as they left our throats but our mother applauded anyway. Our father nodded curtly, then went back to the *New Hanover Gazette*. He set his jaw so his chin stuck out, a sure sign that something wasn't right in his world.

"I think you both show a lot of promise," our mother said.

That night the news was fiery and grim and Addie and I got two scoops of ice cream in our bowls. Chocolate moustaches stained our upper lips. When we showed them to our mother, she could barely even smile.

In those days, when I was eight and Addie was six, we could have passed for twins. But neither of us looked like our mother. She was a regal woman with fox-fur hair and thick plump lips that she dressed in scarlet. She wore high heels while grocery shopping, and even when she changed into slippers at home she walked as if strings were holding her up, with an awareness of self that she didn't seem to have learned so much as simply known.

She hadn't always been so graceful, our father often told us. When they met at an Army mixer, she danced like a duck and he let her know. She walked back to her seat quacking and he followed her. "On our first date, we went ice skating and I got all the bruises" was how he always ended the story; soon enough we were finishing it for him. It seemed like a novelty, our father getting hurt, a man so steely I used to imagine knocking on his leg and hearing armor echo. In the photo from their wedding day they stand together in the city hall lobby, my mother in a flowered dress, my father in a suit, both arms wrapped around her waist, his eyes bright, his face broken by a rare smile. Behind them is a drinking fountain, the only other object in the room.

Our father also said our mother was a woman who didn't always know herself. So perhaps we shouldn't have been surprised when we came in from running drills one morning to hear her announce that she was going to start looking for work. "All the other wives here do something," she explained. "It just doesn't look right, me staying home."

As far as I knew, my mother had never gone to work before, though she had often threatened to do so. None of us seemed to know what she was qualified for, either, and we sat eating breakfast and mulling over the want-ads, my mother's red marker uncapped and ready. I knew she had stuff for cuts that stung like crazy, that she could whistle the opening bars of "Eine kleine Nachtmusik," that she was once the lead baton twirler in her town. But converting these skills to money was another matter, my father said.

Nevertheless, she was determined and, like our father, she couldn't fail at something once she'd begun trying. So every Tuesday and Thursday, after dropping us off at the church, she would go out and perform feats of employability, interviewing anywhere she sensed a spark of interest. And every time she came to pick us up she looked a little more dejected, a little more faded, became a little more difficult to find in the crowd.

But then, we were dejected too. Addie and I still weren't making friends. Even outside of the neighborhood, the other children traveled in preexisting packs. They played games we didn't know the rules to and sang songs we had never heard, songs about fighting the power and sexing people up. At the choir practices they swarmed around each other like bees, their whispers buzzing, their looks barbed. Once when I asked the girl beside me to move her coat, she stood up and saluted me, a sneer singeing her lips. "Yes, drill sergeant," she barked, and the other girls tittered into their fingers.

In the last week of June our mother got a secretary job in a law firm and Marjorie Flox entered our lives. Our father complained that she was a hippie; she was rumored to have made disparaging remarks about Schwarzkopf. But our mother appreciated her "spunk." The night we were told the news, I was carried into my dreams by the magical lilt of her name, which sounded like it belonged to someone who never came out from under a spotlight. The next morning she appeared in our house. She carried a purse the size of a doctor's kit. As the grown-ups got acquainted, Addie and I tried to guess what was in that purse. First she said stuffed animals; then she said board games. I guessed a bugle and told Addie that she'd been hired to play in our yard.

Marjorie Flox was in her late twenties, living on the base alone, her husband having been one of the first deployed. She had a thick waist and a warm manner and I could tell immediately she made my father nervous. We were only just getting used to the house ourselves and she had suddenly filled it up. She moved about us effervescently, in stark contrast to the careful motions of my mother, who tucked us into bed like we were letters being slipped into envelopes. When they were introduced, Marjorie took my father's hand like a man, pumping it up and down with enthusiasm.

"It's so nice to meet you, Walt," she said. "I'm sorry you never got to work with my Harry before he went abroad." I had never heard anyone call my father by his first name, not even my mother. To her he was Dear, to us he was Daddy, and to everyone else he was Sir. The two intimacies so close together—Walt, my Harry—made us all take a step back and hold our breath. Marjorie's hand returned to circling her stomach, as if she were searching for a fortune in it.

"No television," my mother instructed. "Don't take them into town unless I say so."

Chief among my mother's concerns about town was the Veterans' Hall. Addie and I had heard it spoken of in italicized tones by our parents. We had listened carefully. In peacetime it was merely a distraction. They hosted dances that no one attended, potlucks to which no one brought food, movies for shuffling janitors. But in wartime, it had become *a vice*, a place to *stay away from*. We were covertly curious.

"And their lunches are in the fridge," my mother continued. "That's what they'll eat; don't let them tell you otherwise. Girls, be good to Ms. Flox." She cupped both our chins in her two hands, kissed our cheeks, and then followed our father into the new sphere of her life.

Ms. Flox turned to us, a mischievous flash in her eye. "Don't tell your mother, but I don't mind if you call me Marjorie." It seemed a small but precious privilege. I grasped it, said her name all the time, even whispered it to myself when she wasn't in the room.

A blatant disregard for my mother's rules quickly became the norm. It turned out that there was a game in her bag, a Ouija board she had brought from home and hoped would entertain us. At first the concept was baffling; we had never played anything without instructions before. She laid it out on the kitchen table, smoothing it over like she would a bed sheet, and went to pour herself a cup of coffee. We navigated over the letters and numbers with our hands, hovering over the "Yes" and "No" and the ominous "Good-Bye" that lurked at the bottom, dismissing who or what I couldn't say. I felt we had stumbled onto something secret and serious.

"Marjorie, what's an oracle?" I said, pointing to the only word on the board I didn't know.

"Someone with the gift of second sight," she replied. "They can see things that we can't. They can communicate with other realms."

"Realms? What are realms?" Addie asked, the strand of hair she'd been sucking falling from her lips. I hated when she did that; it made me want to pin her to the floor and tie up her hair.

"They're like other worlds, right?" I turned to Marjorie for confirmation. "Like where angels go?"

She set down the planchette and showed us how to position our fingers on it by perching them right at the edge. "Ask it anything you want and it will tell you what it knows."

"You first," Addie said.

"All right. Should I have a cigarette?"

"Marjorie, you can't smoke in here," I said.

"Well, let's just see what the board says."

We gathered above the glass eye and waited to be guided. When the planchette first sparked into action, Addie whimpered. I could feel her fingers shivering, but the movement did not seem to throw the diviner from its path. "Don't be scared," Marjorie said softly. "It's not a question of life and death, after all."

In the end, it proclaimed "Yes" and Marjorie propped herself in an open window. The smoke wreathed itself around her neck, which she offered to the warmth of the sun. Even though I could smell the woody poison of the smoke on her, even though I knew it was bad, I thought she looked glamorous, like she belonged on the cover of a magazine our mother would never buy.

"Do you not play games like this with your friends?"

"Friends?" Addie asked, in the same way she had asked about realms.

"We don't really play with the other kids around here," I said. "I don't think they like us."

"How silly," she said. I didn't know if she meant us or them.

"It's not silly. They're mean. And they make me feel mean too."

She came back to the table, stubbing her cigarette out in the dregs of her coffee so it sizzled. "Don't ever let anyone make you feel something about yourself you don't want to feel," she said. Something flashed across her eyes like a shutter clicking over a camera lens, capturing a moment whose meaning was lost to us. We must not have looked convinced by her words because she changed the subject: "What about a game you two play together?"

Addie and I conferred quickly. Addie wanted to show her the folded paper fortune-teller but I didn't want Marjorie to think we were competing with her. We agreed on light-as-a-feather, stiff-as-a-board.

"Lie still and close your eyes!" Addie instructed.

"I am!" Marjorie squealed.

"Stop wiggling or it won't work," I said. We leaned over her out-stretched form and waited for her face to slacken, her muscles to unravel, her mind to wander. We waited for her to give herself up. Then we wedged our fingers under her body and began lifting. But not actually lifting. Imparting lightness is maybe better. The point, of course, wasn't to lift her but to make her feel as though she was weightless, like she'd just settled into the bottom of a filled tub and the water had made her body an unrecognizable, needless thing.

"Light as a feather, stiff as a board," we chanted in a hushed sing-song. "Light as a feather, stiff as a board." I could feel the rhythm of her breath threading slowly through her ribcage. I could see the creases in her closed eyes, soft as the underside of a dog's ear. I could believe that we were doing something good for her, something more than a game.

"That was nice," she said when we brought her back down.

She let us keep the Ouija board. I hid it behind the crafts box under my bed where my mother no longer bothered to look.

The first week of July marked the start of an extended heat wave. It made us sluggish and cross. We left the mittens to the dust mites and lolled on the sofa in our swimsuits. The leather suctioned to our skin. Outside the soldiers marched with more intensity, as if to beat back the sun itself. "This is nothing," our father reminded us when we slipped into malaise. "Do you know what those boys will have to put up with soon?"

"Dear, don't make a fuss," our mother said. After accepting her new job she had taken to wearing tortoiseshell glasses around the house. Our father looked at her as if he no longer quite recognized her. In hallways they moved to avoid touching one another. Some mornings the couch still held the warmth of his sleeping body. Yet it didn't occur to me to be worried about these developments. I'd never had to before.

Now she took a tiny kerchief from her purse, removed the glasses, and began methodically wiping the lenses. "I know you still see me," he muttered. She spit into the cloth.

On the Fourth of July our father gave a speech about bravery and perseverance against our enemy. But Addie and I couldn't be bothered with that flattened pancake of a country, the one that had the same sound as hacking into a hankie. It was words on a paper, pixels on a television, fear in another child's eyes. We knew we wouldn't lose our father to it and so we forgot it. It wasn't cruelty, it was convenience—luck we had no hand in and could enjoy innocently. We had other things on our minds.

The choir was preparing for our end-of-summer concert. The armpit of the church gave way to the swampy fever of a greenhouse. Our bodies drooped; our voices went limp. Our "Camptown Races" heaved and tumbled on the way out of our mouths. It was in this deteriorating environment that Mr. Giletti announced that there would be a "solo." When he said it, he drew out the last vowel until it became something wholly musical on its own, as if, like the Pied Piper, he hoped to entrance someone into the scheme with his song.

"It's only one line," he pleaded from behind the piano. "Don't make me ask to hear from all of you. I don't think I could quite bear it." But we turned cotton ears to his proposition.

Marjorie came to pick us up at the church that day, hanging back as the mothers streamed forward to collect their sons and daughters. You could tell which ones had recently had husbands shipped off by how white their children's skin got in their grip. The room was filled with the sound of high heels and wet kisses. Once safely paired, the women broke off into gossipy clumps, becoming overgrown versions of their offspring. I was aware of several eyes trailing us as we made our way outside. I went pink in the cheeks as if I'd been slapped with a sunburn. But Marjorie didn't seem to notice.

"I think you should do it, Lucinda," she said, when I told her of the solo. "You have a lovely voice."

I didn't want to seem too flattered in front of Addie, so I said, "When did you ever hear me sing?"

She admitted she hadn't and the next day she brought over her portable record player.

"I know this thing probably seems pretty old," she said. "But I'll bet it's new to you."

It was new to us and it looked like luggage. When she lifted the top, its plastic innards were revealed—the disc of the turntable, the long yellow arm of the spindle, the spinning Oreo cookie dial with its rippled edges.

"What do you want to listen to?" she asked. "I have all sorts of stuff. Most of it's Harry's. He had, *has* a real nostalgia streak."

That day we heard songs about trying a little tenderness and wondering if her hair's still red and feeling so broke up you wanna go home. When a record clicked to a halt, she restarted it until we were singing along with her. In the living room we spun in circles until we staggered to the floor, bull-dozed by dizziness. Marjorie danced in her bare feet, the space between her arches and the floor so large I could slip a finger through it. Her skirt flared out like a bell, and Addie scuttled around behind her, trying to capture the fabric and hide in its folds. I had never seen the underwear of a grown woman before and was surprised to discover that it looked a lot like mine, the flowers faded and boring. I was happy when she collapsed with us on the floor and looked like something else, this time a little porcelain figure that could be propped up on a cake.

"Me and my Harry got married to this song," she said, as she set the next record on. "You know Dusty Springfield? Real name Mary Isabel Catherine Bernadette O'Brien? Wouldn't you like to have four names to choose from like that?"

I agreed I probably would.

"People used to call her bent."

"Bent how?" Addie asked.

"What are you doing the rest of your life?" a voice of velvet purred.

"I don't know," Marjorie answered.

Her eyes seemed very far away from the rest of her. I had an urge to circle my arms around her neck and shake her back into herself. "Marjorie, tell us something about Harry," I said.

"Harry," she murmured. "I was surprised when Harry enlisted. He never seemed to want to do anything grown up. I thought he'd be playing guitar in his band forever. Army boys are supposed to marry generals' daughters. That's what will happen to you two." We wrinkled our noses at the thought.

"I hated when they made him cut his hair," she continued. "He had such beautiful blonde hair." She put two fingers to her lips but there was no cigarette there and she sucked in nothing but air.

"Who made him?" Addie asked.

"The army, dummy." I elbowed her. "They did it to Daddy, too."

"No they didn't. Daddy's hair's always looked like that."

"It'll grow back," Marjorie said.

We nodded. It seemed to be what was called for.

That night, after the records had been packed away and silence had returned to the house, Addie asked our father if Mr. Flox would be coming home soon.

He gazed at her, blank as a clock face, all the mechanics working unseen. "I expect so," he said. Then he went back to flipping vigorously through his newspaper.

My father had rarely induced strong feelings in me before. I had grown used to him not being a warm or affectionate man. He displayed his emotions in gestures as intricate and inflexible as sign language. His idea of a good birthday was a home cooked meal and an early bedtime. But that night, for the first time, I hated him. It was a childish hate and mostly gone by morning, but the taste of it lingered, like something sour you can't scrape away no matter how far back your toothbrush goes.

After consulting the Ouija board, I volunteered for the solo the next day.

"We should do something to celebrate," Marjorie said when I told her my news. "What if we went on a little trip?"

It was a lazy day in late July, the sort that feels already over before the sun's even come up. The three of us were in the kitchen, poking at the waffles Marjorie had defrosted for lunch. I was preoccupied with cutting mine into four perfect wedges, so it was Addie who answered, "We aren't supposed to go on trips. Mom said."

"No?" Marjorie said. "Not even a little one?"

She took a drag from her cigarette and pursed her lips into a ring, puffing the smoke out in little O's. She stuck her finger through one and when she twirled it, the smoke broke apart and crept into the air. Addie giggled.

"Where do you want to go, Marjorie?" I asked as I dribbled the syrup up to the rims of the waffle's honeycombs.

"Have you girls ever been to the Veterans' Hall?"

I had to pinch Addie under the table to keep her from shouting. No kid on the base had ever gone to the hall before, but all of them wanted to. If we went, we'd be more sought out than the ones who knew things about sex.

Marjorie didn't have a car, so we had to walk into town. Addie and I had taken the trip before but never on foot. It was a world we had only seen from backseats, the buildings and people shuttling by us like scenery in a movie instead of a recognizable part of our lives. As far as our parents were concerned, there was "home" and the "place to go," and nothing important in between. Forming attachments to grocery stores and bakeries was dangerous; transfers to other bases loomed just out of sight.

With Marjorie the journey was leisurely. Once the sounds of the soldiers faded and the streets straightened out of our cul-de-sac formation, it was easy to believe we were coming from somewhere else. In town we walked with the purposelessness that signaled authority. We stooped to pet dogs. We smiled at strangers. We jaywalked.

"The hall is just at the next corner," Marjorie said, taking our hands and steering us to a building that had the wan color and dimpled texture of oatmeal. There were no windows and only one entrance; it had all the invitational qualities of a Cold War–era bunker. In the excitement, my heart went ahead of me through the door.

It was a single room, dark and clotted with smoke. Ceiling fans sliced the air above but couldn't coerce it into movement. Along one wall ran a bar with a few patrons slumped over it, pulling from beers and talking quietly with one another. Our parents didn't keep liquor in the house and I was entranced by the bottles lined up like perfume in a department store, promising something precious and sweet. Opposite was a pool table, the felt shedding in green tufts. Three men stood around it, leaning on their cues. In the back was a taciturn jukebox and, hovering just behind it, the outspread arms of an American flag. It was odd and familiar and it gave me a little thrill to see it.

Two of the men at the bar had turned toward us, and one of them waved to Marjorie. He had a bald head and a full mustache as if he'd licked his lips while cutting his hair and it'd all gotten stuck there. He was plump in the face and his belly was wrestling to break out of his shirt.

"He looks like a walrus," Addie whined. "A big beached walrus." Marjorie put a finger to her lips, then led us over to be introduced.

"Lucinda, Addie. This is Eben. He's an old friend of mine," she said.

The man wiped his hand over his flannel, then offered it to me. When I shook it, his fingers wrapped all the way to my wrist. But his grip was gentle and he let go as if he were setting a small animal free. Then he did the same to Addie, who hadn't taken her eyes from his mustache since we'd come over. He wiggled it at her and winked.

"Where'd you find these two, Margie?"

It was the other man talking, the one with the hair cut so short it was the same pale pink as his scalp. Without quite knowing why, I was surprised when he turned around and didn't have a scar on his face. Something in his voice suggested damage.

"Out on the obstacle course. They made it halfway up the climbing wall before I caught them."

"That's a tough wall to climb. Undone many a good man," he replied, but there was no mirth in his voice.

"Girls, this is Tex," Marjorie said.

"Like the state?" Addie asked.

He nodded. "But I was born in California."

"Really?" Addie said. "What's the capital?"

"Couldn't be bothered to learn it."

"Are you in the army?"

"I'm shipping out next week."

"So you're not a veteran yet."

I pinched Addie in the meat of her upper arm but Tex had already turned his head toward Marjorie and was speaking something low in her ear.

"What about you?" Addie asked Eben, as she rubbed the little red nicks back into her skin. "Are you in the army?"

"I was," Eben said. His voice was soft and warm and seemed to issue from someplace deep inside him. "In Vietnam. A long time ago."

"Were you a general? Our daddy was a general."

"Nope. Just a grunt."

"That's a funny thing to be," Addie said.

"I suppose it is," Eben said. "Would you girls like anything to drink?"

I looked over at Marjorie and saw she was drinking from Tex's glass. It was holding liquid honey. "Can we have that?" I pointed.

Eben didn't even turn around. "What about lemonade? I know Hal always keeps some around." He nodded to the man behind the bar. By the time he'd helped us both onto the stools beside him, there were two large glasses in front of us.

"Careful," the bartender said. "That's stronger stuff than a lot of the liquor we've got."

"Thanks, Hal," Eben said, looking toward us and nodding his head.

"Thanks, Hal," we murmured. The drink was cool and tart and each sip did a dance across my tongue.

"You know what they say, right?" Eben continued. "When life gives you lemons . . ."

"Squirt the juice in life's eye," Tex said. Then, as he went to rest his arm out on the bar, he brushed Marjorie's hair with his fingertip. The strands shivered in his wake like a wind chime in a soft breeze.

"Why aren't you girls in school?" Eben asked.

"It's summer," I said. It was torture to look away from Marjorie, to put my eyes on him.

"Don't you know that?" Addie asked. "Don't you have kids?"

"My kids are grown and gone," Eben said.

"Where to?" Addie asked.

"Well, one went to New York and one went to Florida. They split ways, I guess. You will too."

"I'll never leave," Addie said.

"No," Eben replied. "It's the duty of the young to leave things behind. Especially places like this."

"You didn't leave," Addie huffed.

"You're right. But I didn't go anywhere else neither."

"I will," I said. But it was a promise to me, not to him.

Marjorie let out that high shriek of a laugh, the one somewhere between joy and desperation. The balls snapped at one another on the pool table. Hal swabbed soapy circles onto the bar with a dishcloth. Eben gave us each a dollar to put in the jukebox. We were tall enough to reach the buttons but not to see the records, so he dragged over a stool for us.

It must have happened then, while we were flipping through the discs. As Addie fed her money into the black plastic tongue, I glanced over and saw Tex grab Marjorie by the wrist. He seemed to be saying something: "Cut it out." The look in her eyes was the kind you'd give an animal that had backed you into a corner, warning and pleading and tempting all at once, and the sight of it made me turn quickly away. When I glanced over again they were gone.

"Eben?" I cried, flailing my arms in the general direction of the empty bar. But he simply stood there, tongue pushing a toothpick to the other side of his mouth. I insisted on being lifted off the stool before my selection was made. Once back on the ground, I performed a quick reconnaissance of the hall. I checked both bathrooms but only found strange scribbling in the stalls, drawings of foreign anatomy, numbers scratched out and initials enshrined in hearts, the name "Jenny" in several compromising suggestions. I snuck a peek behind the bar but only Hal's slacks and loafers were moving about back there. I even crouched beneath the pool table before returning to Eben and Addie in leaky tears.

"Don't fret," Eben said. "They'll be back soon."

"We're. Not. Supposed. To separate," I managed between gasps.

"We're not supposed to be here in the first place," Addie said. "Let's get you another lemonade."

Eben sat with us for a full half-hour. He spoke of some things that I barely remember. About the rubbery turkey they served in the army and how it had spoiled Thanksgiving for him forever, a quirk I had believed to belong to my father alone and resented Eben for ruining. About the only Vietnamese word he ever learned: dung lai, for stop. About his daughter and her fruitless pursuit of a singing career.

"Lucinda likes to sing, too," Addie piped up. "She has a solo in the choir soon."

"Can I hear it?" Eben asked, his voice timid as a child's, as if he hoped we would speak as equals. But my misery would not allow a single note.

Addie had just complained that she needed to pee when Marjorie returned, alone. Her mouth was drawn tight as a keyhole. The hair at the nape of her neck was knotted, as if a fist had weaved through it. She might have been crying. She walked by without acknowledging us and slipped into the ladies room. Addie sighed and went to follow her but Eben clamped a hand on Addie's shoulder.

"Better give her a minute," he said.

It was five minutes before Marjorie reappeared, her hand circling her stomach in that odd way she had, her hair curled fetal on her head. I wanted to run to her, fasten myself to her waist, bury my nose in the cotton bouquet of her dress. But when we went to her, she simply took our hands and led us outside. We were greeted by violent sunshine and the birds going on about something or other.

The next day, quite suddenly, was the last day of July, the last good day of any summer. After that it was one quick slide from August into the schoolyard. Addie and I came down for breakfast and found our parents waiting in the kitchen. They were seated next to each other, facing forward, hands clasped in little discrete temples on the table. My mother was wearing her glasses and the sun cast white circles over her eyes. Neither of them spoke and I wondered for a moment if they'd seen us, if maybe we couldn't sneak back upstairs. But then my father said, "Sit down, girls."

Addie stuffed a strand of hair into her mouth and we took the chairs across from them. My mother removed her glasses and pinched the skin at the bridge of her nose. My father was staring into the cavern of his hands, which still carried the tang of the aftershave he'd slapped on his face an hour ago.

"Are we having breakfast?" Addie asked.

"In a minute," our father said. "We need to talk with you."

"Is Marjorie coming back?" I asked.

"This is not about Marjorie," our mother said, bringing her glasses to the table with a thunk. Her words put up fences I couldn't see over.

They told us about the trial separation, that they would be sleeping in separate "quarters," as my father called them, but would remain in the same house for the sake of "appearances," as my mother put it. Addie would be moved into my bedroom that night. I'm not sure which news upset us more. Neither was up for discussion.

After morning drills we were walked over to Mrs. Brewster's house next door and we watched from an unfamiliar window as our parents drove off to work. We knew the Brewster children from the choir. Angela was imperfectly reliable when it came to gossip but she still liked to give it with gusto. Brian was even younger than Addie; all he liked was making train engine sounds. Mrs. Brewster served us peppered eggs that had the gray quality of brain matter.

"Oh you poor things. I can't imagine," she clucked. "What was that woman thinking?"

I didn't know who she meant but she had the sort of wobbly face that inspired argument. "We'll be fine," I said. But that no longer seemed a certainty. I said it again anyway.

That night Addie and I boycotted dinner. We let our potatoes turn spongy and our milk grow skin and we were sent to bed early. We sat and listened as their voices rumbled beneath us. The room seemed suddenly smaller with Addie in it. We were like twins, though not ones that looked alike or conjoined in any particular place. I had treasured the time apart that bedtime once afforded. I wanted to push her into the closet. I wanted to take her in my arms.

"I hate Mommy," she said.

"I hate Daddy more," I said. For some reason, we both started giggling. We couldn't stop. We covered our mouths and let the laughter bubble out of our hands. When we finally caught our breath, we noticed it had gone quiet downstairs. We didn't know if that was a good sign or a bad one.

"Do you think they'll go to court?" Addie asked. "Do you think they'll make us choose?"

We only knew one boy whose parents had split up, on the last base we'd lived on. He'd announced it to the rest of us just like that: they were "splitting up." I'd imagined the earth beneath their house cracking in two. I imagined the eyes of their windows turning sad as the ground swallowed them up in its great grassy maw. Instead they began fighting over his custody. At first, he was boastful. *His* parents were fighting over who loved him the most, he claimed. Then one day he simply disappeared. The house was put up for sale a week later. We never found out who won. But we could safely agree it wasn't him.

I said the only thing I could think of: "Let's ask the board."

The Ouija board had already collected a considerable amount of dust. I sneezed as I pulled it out from under my bed. Somehow I hoped it would look different. That I wouldn't have to search for an answer, that one would just present itself to me. But the same "Yes" and "No" and "Good-Bye" taunted me.

Addie and I took our positions over the board. We placed our fingers on the planchette and closed our eyes. We chanted the question and awaited movement. Slowly it began its survey. It crept first one way and then the other before turning back again. It circled its target and then it stopped. We counted breathlessly to three and looked together. It rested on the letter "X." I thought that was definitely a "No." Addie declared it a stupid game.

That night, as Addie and I fell asleep, as she burrowed her nose into me as if I was her napkin, I thought of the photograph of my parents on their wedding day. I had always thought my mother looked shy at being caught in the arms of my father, her gaze cast away from the camera, her teeth nipping at the pulp of her lips. But now I knew it was the same look I'd seen in Marjorie's eyes that afternoon at the hall. It was that look of resignation, which I could recognize but not name, in many of the women around me that summer. It was the knowledge of doing the difficult thing without knowing if it was the right one. It was jumping from the burning building while the firemen were still locating their tarp.

Two days later we went to war. The base rattled with an agitated silence. The flags stretched across the front porches. The children were kept indoors. Two weeks later the choir had its first and only concert of the summer. The four of us went together to the church and as I watched my mother and father greeting the other families, I wondered if what they were doing would be considered a sin. If they would be struck down now or later, together or separately. I looked for Marjorie but she wasn't there.

Mr. Giletti was in a hand-wringing state. He stood before the piano and as each child arrived, he quickly shuffled them into formation on the risers. We were all outfitted like little adults, the girls in dresses that usually stayed shelved until Christmas, the boys' hair combed into wet helmets. There was a microphone set up and when I came near, Mr. Giletti adjusted it to my height. "You remember the line?" he asked, his pupils thickened by a pre-performance glaze. I nodded and as I made my way to my place I repeated it in my head. I bet my money on a bobtail nag. I *bet* my money on a bobtail nag. I bet *my money* on a bobtail nag.

The program was heavy on Americana. The country was beautiful and the banner was star-spangled and the soldiers came marching home. Finally, after it was agreed that this land was both your land and mine, it was time for "Camptown Races."

We started well enough. I could pluck out individual voices on either side of me but I couldn't tell how we sounded. It didn't matter; only mine would be heard alone. But when I got down to the microphone, I found the words had escaped from me. I heard the singers behind me reach their crest. Mr. Giletti held the chord and looked to me. The silence swelled into a pillow I wanted to clutch over my ears. The electricity of the microphone buzzed beneath my lips. I saw my parents paying dutiful attention in the crowd, just like all the other couples, and felt an anger blister in me. What was this fluency for fooling others that all adults seemed to have? Where did it come from? And when would I get it? I opened my mouth and out came the only words I could think of: "What are you doing the rest of your life?" Then my knees locked up and I collapsed on the floor.

I only sing in the shower now, but singing was not the only thing that didn't last through that summer. Marjorie never came to care for us again, though we did see her periodically around the neighborhood. We watched as her belly ballooned out. Then a few months later we watched her push a stroller down her drive. A few months after that, her Harry returned to her and the three of them moved to another town. By the time our soldiers began pulling out of Iraqi territories, my parents had officially separated and Addie and I were living with our mother on civilian grounds. She got promoted from secretary to paralegal. We wore jeans to school and bought hot lunches. That spring I turned nine and got my first Walkman. We saw our father every other weekend and on holidays.

My mother says he reached me first that day in the church. I don't remember. Nor, really, does it matter. I came to slowly, the lights so bright they almost blinded me back into darkness. Then my father and mother and Addie began winking into shape above me, all of them lifting me up from the ground as though I weighed absolutely nothing at all.

THE MODERN AGE

Cleavage

When Dr. Rob told Nan Gordon she would have to have her left breast removed, she decided she would sleep with him. He needed to know just what he was taking from her. She needed to know too.

Nan was startled but not surprised when she found the lump. She'd been warned of the possibility before, of the cancerous rogue that had wound its way through her genetic code. She'd seen the demonstration slides of excised tissue, sectioned and veined like a halved orange, the tumor nestled in the fat like overstuffed pith. But it always seemed like something so far away from her daily concerns, something unseen she could put off, like taxes or grad school. Now, in this deliberately inoffensive exam room, indignant in her flower-patterned gown, bare ass pinching the paper beneath her, the knowledge was inescapable: she had no one to blame but herself.

Dr. Rob was in his mid-thirties, with a thin hoop hanging limply through his left lobe and a face unwrinkled by the bad news he had to give. He was a robot, a robot with woolly arms, and his insistence on maintaining both the formality of "Doctor" and the casualness of "Rob" infuriated Nan.

"What do you do with them?" she asked.

"Our patients? We—

"No," she said, "My breast. What do you do with it after you cut it loose?"

He seemed surprised by the question, the indifferent mask of his face sliding southward. He recovered with admirable agility. "Well," he said, tapping his pen against his lip. "First you have to sign the specimen over to the hospital. Then we do what we want with it."

Even when he was joking his voice had all the variety and warmth of a heart monitor. Nan didn't know if she liked him or hated him. "What does that mean?"

"Depending on our needs, sometimes we use it for testing," he said. "And sometimes we incinerate it."

She hated him.

He began droning about the procedure, how her breast wouldn't literally be separated whole from her body like some tribal ritual. But she was no longer listening. Instead she fixated on her face in the mirror floating above his right shoulder. Under the harsh fluorescent light her skin took on a subterranean tone. She looked like something set out on a slab, formaldehyde worming its way through her veins, wedging into her organs. In mere minutes she'd lost years of being beautiful.

"I think we should discuss how you'll be feeling after the operation. Sexually, I mean." He looked at her and smiled an insurance salesman grin, bright and cheery and attempting to hide the grit of his teeth, the boredom behind his eyes. She imagined his tongue flicking back and forth behind that wall of immaculate bone. Then she imagined him flicking that tongue against the tip of the nipple he would soon be taking from her.

"If we must," she said.

"I know I don't seem like an expert. But I've talked many women through this. Now, for a while you'll probably be feeling uncomfortable with your body, somewhat unfeminine, incomplete."

"Plus the other one will be lonely."

"Nobody to hang out with," he said, trying to match her tone.

She stared at him until her eyes burned, until the silence between them became so crushing she imagined it knocking out all his dainty molars.

"Yes. Well," he continued, flipping through the chart to avoid any more direct contact, "it may be some time before you feel like being intimate with someone again. But these feelings shouldn't last."

"How long?"

"I'm not a shrink; I can't tell you that. It's going to depend entirely on your own recovery process. But you're twenty-eight and otherwise healthy. And you're only in stage one. Plus I'm sure you have family to support you."

"Some," she answered. She thought of her mother, Pippa, waiting in the lobby, burying her cigarette cravings in a copy of *Dog Fancy*, and felt suddenly, overwhelmingly tired. Dr. Rob must have noticed because his voice softened, not in kindness so much as acknowledgment of what was required.

"This is a loss," he said. "And given your age, it's perfectly normal to mourn. Many women feel that way. Let me give you the names of some support groups that meet in the area." She took them down. Three hours later she met him at his apartment. The sex was smooth and spotless and over before either of them had gotten their clothes off.

This, in its way, was its own act of mourning: the first sex Nan had in over a year and she could easily imagine it being the last she ever did. After so many sloppy attempts at intimacy and so much time spent sleepwalking through the motions, she could keep her body to herself now. This was its fond farewell, its kerchief wave from a departing ship deck. And now it was all over. It was lying in bed with a man she didn't even like.

"So," Dr. Rob said afterward, "should we see each other again?"

"I think we have to," she said.

"Oh, right." He gave a sad sort of laugh.

She turned her back to him and he did not reach for her. They curled away from each other and the cold rushed in to fill the empty space. The next week she requested a transfer to Dr. Sophie Hargrove, whose eyebrows came together in sympathetic V's and who never, ever joked about other people's breasts. She had the operation a week after that.

Pippa's apartment was a hospice for cigarettes; they were nursed to the very end. It took Nan several days of her scheduled convalescence to realize her mother wasn't looking for her when she said, "Oh, there you are," picking through butts in the nearest ashtray like a raccoon through trash. Every time it happened, Nan felt she'd stayed too long.

Nan woke every morning to these smoke-stained fingers reaching for her mouth, as Pippa shoved a quickie cocktail of codeine and orange juice down her throat before heading to work. Once Nan was certain that her mother had left for the day, she would spend several minutes screaming her throat raw. After this, she usually got sick. Then she spent her afternoons watching soaps. When she closed her eyes, shoulder pads and push-up bras swam in the darkness. She got used to the sight of the ceiling above her, could recognize its kinks and whorls even at night. The days passed too slowly, like stones through a kidney. She could feel herself growing rotten.

She certainly looked rotten. Every time she changed her bandage she found something newly fearsome underneath. The stitches were the worst: the skin pulled tight, bound together with thick black string, a nest of spiders instead of a breast. The longer she looked, the more difficult it became to remember her body in other times: at the prom, encased in terrible teal tulle; camping at the lake, shuddering against the fleece of a sleeping bag; leaning against the wall of a nightclub, sleek and solid and aware of how substantial it was. This was what she knew now: her body strung up like a violin, ready to be locked away in velvet lining, far from the dangers of dust motes and sympathy.

She tried to go to the support meetings, but she never got past the doorway. All the downcast and wrinkled faces, the bare heads covered in bright paisley scarves, the bodies that seemed to cave in like cored apples. It was everything that she didn't want to be reminded she could become, that she suspected she already had become. This pain was her own, not something that could be focus-grouped away. So whenever she saw a smiling, sunken-eyed woman making her way toward her, Nan would turn quickly to the bulletin board and grab the nearest flyer, turning back and waving it with a shrug. She put them on Pippa's refrigerator, so she was bombarded every day: *Stop Smoking! Quit Drinking! Why Can't I Control My Cravings? Why Is My Penis Sad?* All those problems and all those questions, when all she wanted to know was how to feel supported when she didn't really feel anything.

Then one day Nan woke up and felt something where it didn't belong. She walked into the chilled air of the bathroom and underneath her robe she felt her nipples rise. In the mirror before her only one breast stood out against the plush white folds. The left side of her remained neutral, reclusive. Yet, unmistakably, she could feel both breasts on her, could feel the soft slopes suspending, the right one always a little heavier than its twin. Nan removed the robe.

Since she'd had the stitches removed, the scar tissue had spread across the wound like clay poured in a mold. Now her left chest looked as if she had been excavated. But she could feel a breast there. She put her hands down and closed her eyes, tried to envision her body as she knew it was. As though it recognized what she was doing, her invisible breast began furiously to itch. Well,

Nan thought. That settles things. Somehow it had found its way back to her again.

The itch remained all day, building from a mild sizzle under the skin to a steady blaze. By noon Nan had to put on mittens to keep from clawing at her chest. By three she had emptied the apartment of antihistamines. She stretched out on the couch, pulled the covers up to her chin, and half-expected to die. Instead, she woke up at seven to the smell of smoke and meatloaf commingling in the air.

Pippa sat at the kitchen table, still in her scrubs, her upper half enrobed in a gaudy approximation of van Gogh's *Sunflowers*. Nan took the empty chair opposite her and Pippa scooted a plate in her direction. She cut a thick brown slab from the loaf and used an ice cream scoop to serve the mashed potatoes. But Nan wouldn't eat it; she would just push it around.

"My God, what a day I've had," said Pippa, her voice strained like weak tea. "Third sixteen-year-old mother of the week. Third premature birth. It's goddamn depressing." She lit a cigarette. "Why are you wearing mittens?"

Nan looked up at her mother and was startled to realize how close in appearance they had grown over the last few weeks. Though Pippa had Nan when she was eighteen, there had always seemed a safe distance between them. Her mother had carried the weariness of old age even in her youth. Now that weariness manifested in the loose yellow knitting of Pippa's skin, the bird's wings poised for flight in the corners of her eyes, the collarbone that stuck up from her body like a salute. Nan recognized these as her own. She felt the first tell-tale pricking of the itch and shuddered. Then she reached out and plucked the cigarette from her mother's fingers.

"Would you quit with that, please?" Nan asked, as she stubbed it out on the rim of her plate.

"Well, you're not giving me much choice, are you?"

"You think it can't happen twice in one family?"

"What's gotten into you?"

She had spoken with concern but Nan could sense the disappointment that lingered just behind it. She was a bad patient. Something in her had failed. She didn't have to say anything for Pippa to know it. She left her mother to her thoughts, to the wilted cigarette, to the babies that could be cupped in her hands, confident that this bad day would soon be replaced by another.

"It's there!" Nan insisted to Dr. Hargrove at their next appointment.

"What's there?"

"My breast," she said. "My breast is back."

"You know," Dr. Hargrove said, "this is a relatively common occurrence. In almost half the cases, actually. No different from an amputee with a phantom limb."

Amputee. Nan's bones went brittle at the very word. Amputees were for twenty-four-hour news coverage and war movies; they were human-interest stories, heroes. They were rebuilt with metal; their bodies became bionic. She had no such hope.

"Let's check your progress," Dr. Hargrove said. "Tell me if it hurts."

She began rubbing her finger over the grooves of the scar, as if it were a palm she could read a fortune in. Nan didn't know whether to be shocked by the suddenness of the gesture or the coldness of the doctor's skin, which penetrated the thin plastic sheath of her gloves. Nan felt the ripple of a wedding ring and tried to imagine the type of man Dr. Hargrove would marry. A weak one, certainly, as most married men were or became. Perhaps an old patient she had somehow been persuaded to cure for life.

Abruptly Dr. Hargrove peeled off her gloves and dropped them in a biohazard bin. The future, it seemed, was not promising. "Well, you didn't mention any pain, which is a good sign," she said. Nan felt that old scrape of fear in her stomach that she used to get when she was called on to give an answer in school. Was there supposed to be pain? Was there pain she had missed? Could she take the test over again?

That night the itch returned and then refused to leave. Nan knew she was being punished for her unpleasantness. She pled with the vengeful breast. She tried babying it, rubbing the area with a cloth and powdering it. When that didn't work she grew angry, threatened it. Once she stood in front of the mirror, holding a pen knife, not to reopen the wound but to test the apparition above. Finally she could do nothing else but lie on the couch and try to ignore the friction of the fabric against the breast that stirred but would not wake.

The next day Nan picked up the phone and heard Dr. Rob. "How are you?" he asked. Then he added, "I've been meaning to call."

"Why? You're not my doctor."

"I know that."

Nan felt that combination of lethargy and curiosity that was always aroused by calls from bad dates. The men were no longer of interest to her but their reasons for contacting her were and she approached them studiously. She assumed they'd found the evening as terrible as she did. She wondered what she'd done to encourage them.

"What is it?"

"I'd like to see you again."

It did not seem she was being asked.

Nan was out of practice at being presentable. On the day of the date she didn't fiddle too much with her hair, hoping to stave off its loss a little longer. She was already beginning to look like one of those sad-eyed dolls whose owner has washed, cut, and combed her plastic mane beyond repair. She rouged her cheeks, mascaraed her eyes, perfumed her neck to mask her medical scent. But she didn't want to look perfect. She wanted to look like herself, or at least the self she remembered once being. Finally she slipped the falsie in, that fleshy pad that gripped her like a hand and made her feel like a teenager grappling in a backseat. She grimaced as she felt it struggle for control over its invisible, unyielding rival. Once the breast had quieted she was ready.

She heaved a small sigh of relief when she opened the front door. Dr. Rob didn't look perfect either. There was still the same thin hoop, the same shock of black arm hair only half-hidden by his rolled up sleeves. Out of the harsh florescence of the exam room he no longer seemed robotic. Instead there was something wolfish about him, but not in any sense that made her want to back away. He clutched a small bundle of peonies to his chest, so excessive and arterial red that it looked like a beating heart.

"Could you eat?" he asked, as they made their way to the car.

The question startled Nan. In the months after the operation she had treated her meals with the same structured disinterest as an anorexic. She would eat but there were rules. No eating where she slept, for example. It reminded her too much of the hospital. She could eat meat but nothing flesh-colored. Fish was tricky and she'd given up on chicken completely. No, she couldn't eat, not in front of him. He peered at her now and it took her a moment to realize it was because she had stopped moving.

"Drinks then?"

Nan was still on her pain medication and hadn't had alcohol in several months. She wasn't quite sure what it would do to her. But she liked the possibilities this offered.

"I think I could do that," she said.

"I know a bar near here. We can walk to it."

The walk was about eight minutes. It took them ten to find something to talk about. It was the first warm day of spring; people were shedding things all over. Side by side on the street, moving past parents with baby strollers and intensely sweating joggers, conscious of the closeness of their bodies, it was easy to believe better things were pushing them forward.

It was not a romantic place. The music was loud, the lighting infernal. Seated over two glasses of wine it was impossible to ignore how little they had to say and it was an effort not to just sit and appraise one another. Nan felt like she was doing a bad impersonation of herself. A cruise ship comedian, two drink minimum. She took a long sip of her wine. It went down like cough syrup and settled on her stomach like a balm.

Dr. Rob filled the space with perfectly timed fingernail taps on his glass. Nan felt it reverberate in the nerves of her teeth. She bit down on her tongue and felt the shock travel half the length of her spine before it branched off and fizzled out in the dull lumps of her breasts. She must have winced because he stopped and asked, "Is something wrong?"

"No." She put a hand to her head and when she pulled away several strands of hair came with it. She shook them free quickly, hoping he hadn't noticed. They drifted to the floor, to be picked up and carried off on someone else's clothes.

"This feels weird, doesn't it? I mean, it's not really our first date," he said. "It's not even a date. Is it?"

"You called me. I'm not going to define it."

"Fair enough. Better that we don't, anyway."

"Don't what?"

"Define it," he replied. "Do you need another?"

Instantly a burst of warm clouds filled her head. "Please," she said.

As he turned to order another round, Nan noticed the fingernail he had finally stilled. Caught in the light, she could see that it was bisected by a thick half-moon scar. Nan reached over and ran her thumb over the defective nail. The mark was smooth. It had merged with the rest of his body. He jumped at her touch but she had already retreated.

"What happened there?" she asked.

"My brother caught it in a window when I was twelve," he said, running his own finger over it as if he hoped to rub it away. "I cried. And never heard the end of it. Doesn't look so bad now, though. I've seen worse."

Nan felt something snap inside but it was too quick for her to recognize what it was.

"So have I," she said. She was already drunk; she could tell by the way the words fell from her tongue like lemmings off a cliff, each one a little heavier and quicker to die. "I assume this injury has been the most significant moment of your life?"

"That's a pretty ridiculous assumption, don't you think?"

"Well, I'm making it anyway." She took another sip of her wine and this time her phantom breast scrambled under its viscous weight, like something fighting to keep its head above water.

"Significance in life is overrated," Dr. Rob said. "If we're going by the life markers that everyone else considers important, I've already hit them all. I got married too young, was divorced before I graduated college. I went to medical school, like my mother wanted. Then she died. But I'd like to think I still have other things to do."

Nan was terrible at meeting other people's mothers. She always felt she was intruding on something, had dug herself into some private burrow of mother and son she didn't know the way out of. She never got the jokes. She never properly appreciated the meal. It made Nan think she was sleeping with a stranger.

"What did she die of?"

"Cancer," he said.

"Breast?"

"Throat. You ever hear someone who's had their voice box removed? It's like listening to someone who's already died."

The bartender was lingering by their emptied drinks. Dr. Rob made a curt gesture toward him as if he were dismissing an over-eager dog. Nan didn't like the way he was looking at her now, with the same sterile concern that had accompanied her first prognosis.

"Listen," he said. "I understand. I know how something like this can come to define your life. I know it defined my mother's."

"I'm not dying."

"You're lucky. But I don't think it's healthy to ignore how close you came."

Nan grew so angry that she was almost giddy. Her left breast seethed right along with her. She felt it swelling, as if it had been stung by a hundred wasps. "Look," she said, "I'm sorry about your mother. But losing her doesn't mean you know more about grief."

"No. But being a doctor does give me some insight into the process."

"If you didn't call me as a doctor, then please don't talk to me as one. You're not very good at it."

"Right now I'm trying to remember why I called in the first place."

He drained his glass in one gulp. Nan watched his Adam's apple bob, a common enough occurrence but one she so rarely observed that it felt intimate. She had the sudden urge to reach out and stroke his throat. Typical of her, to notice his handsomeness only in his resentment. She was always noticing the good things at the wrong times. Looking at him now, she ached in unexpected places.

"I think we should go," Dr. Rob said. He sat with his shoulders hunched up to his ears. She could have knocked him over with a toothpick if she'd wanted. And he probably would have stayed down.

The walk back to the apartment was even quieter than the one to the bar. At the door, he brushed her cheek with his and shook her hand. He didn't say it was nice or that they would do it again soon, because it wasn't and they wouldn't. In the morning, she found she had scratched at her scar in her sleep. Her fingers were crusted with blood.

At their next appointment, Dr. Hargrove tried to make Nan's breast disappear. Nan pressed her body against a full-length freestanding mirror, her naked chest bisected by the glass, as the doctor moved her right breast in a slow, determined circle. They were tricking her brain, Dr. Hargrove said. The itch would subside if her body believed the lost breast had returned to her. But first, her brain would have to see it.

Nan tried to keep her gaze fixed on the image in the mirror as she'd been instructed and not on the obscuring glint coming off Dr. Hargrove's glasses, the jaw she clenched to stifle a yawn. She had the sour-sweet smell of overripe cherries. It came overwhelmingly from her embossed red lips. They had never been this close before. There had always been a desk or something else between them.

"Do you feel any change yet?" Dr. Hargrove asked, indicating with her eyes Nan's irritated left side as she continued to massage the right. Nan tilted her neck to better see her cupped breast below her, the nipple tipped upward like the nose of a curious dog, and beside it, that same breast reflected in the mirror, a bobbing double, a weightless simulacrum.

But she couldn't concentrate. She kept wondering what would happen if a nurse walked in, if Dr. Hargrove would blush and pull away from her like a man would or nod, smile, and continue on with the business at hand. Nan had never felt less sexual and more exposed in her life.

"Are you ready?" Dr. Hargrove didn't wait for an answer before taking Nan's right hand and placing it where her own had just been.

Her instinct was to knead the breast like she was searching for the knot of another tumor. Eventually she found a rhythm that was close enough to pleasing to keep steady. But it was useless. Every time the phantom breast seemed close to being lulled, it flared up again. The flesh and fat beneath her hand remained stubbornly inert.

"I don't think it's working," Nan said after a few more minutes of spiritless rolling and lifting.

"Maybe if you had a partner?"

Nan looked down the length of the mirror, at the wan frozen lump on the right and the jagged pink stripe on the left, and felt a great wave of exhaustion break over her. Looking back on all her friends of the past few years, she remembered bodies and grasped for names, recalled arguments and forgot the people involved. She knew everyone in halves and, she suspected, by the halves not worth knowing. They'd done what she'd asked at the time, to leave her alone. She could hardly ask more of them now.

Nan returned to her apartment and to work at the local TV station. Her coworkers, smug-looking women who clung to past grievances and circled her like sharks, gave her cards and bright pink balloons. "Like the ribbon," one of the anchorwomen said. Nan put typos in the teleprompter. The itch remained.

She gave the mirror therapy a few half-hearted tries but every time she pressed her body against the glass, her left side would grow unmanageable, clawing and clinging like a fidgety child she couldn't set back on the ground. Instead she indulged herself in fantasies of stripping naked in public places, in front of children and elderly couples, of laughing and weeping as they looked away or covered her up.

One day Nan went to Pippa's apartment for dinner and saw a "Cancer Free!" banner taped up in the kitchen. Her mother sat alone at the table, her hands palms down on the wood as if she were trying to steady herself. "I quit smoking last week," she announced. "But I'm still trying to figure out what else to do with my hands."

"What about knitting?"

"Too matronly. I could see myself buying a little dog though. Let it sit on my lap, stroke it whenever I got the urge."

"That could be good therapy, actually. As long as you didn't end up strangling it."

"I'm trying gum right now," she said, opening her mouth to reveal a mushy pearl tucked in her teeth.

"You look good, Pippa," Nan said, and after she did, she realized it was true. Something warm had settled under Pippa's skin. Indeed, despite her stance, everything about her seemed to have settled. Her shoulders were looser, her eyes were sharper; she even smelled better. And her calmness had seeped its way into the room itself. Without all the ashtrays around, it seemed somehow less breakable.

"I don't think I've looked this good since I stopped seeing your father," Pippa said. "He hated smoking. I think I started doing it as a way to justify leaving him. I could smoke. What freedom! Men make us do such stupid things."

"I didn't know that," Nan said.

"Oh don't worry," Pippa said, reaching out to pat her hand. "You seem to have avoided stupidity so far. I'm proud of you."

"For that?"

"Among other things," she said.

When Nan called Dr. Rob to ask him on another date, his initial response was "I don't think I want to." His voice had taken on the taut, wounded timbre of a spoiled child.

"Well, do you think or do you know?"

"Well," he countered, "what did you have in mind?"

"Whatever you want," she promised. "My treat."

When the day arrived, Nan prepared with less fastidiousness than before. The only ritual she truly relished partaking in was the setting of the falsie, whose usual pinch and protest made her prematurely nostalgic for when the phantom breast would be gone.

Dr. Rob chose a torridly Italian place, fraught with candlelight and bas-reliefs, and ordered the third most expensive thing on the menu. Nan avoided his face and watched as he cut his steak into egalitarian cubes. After chewing and swallowing each individual piece, he would take a sip of his water and swish it around in his mouth. She felt the itch returning, a darting pin never pricking in the same place. She wondered if he was being deliberately irritating.

"I went into remission, you know," she said, as the waitress set down two cups of coffee.

He pulled two sugar packets from the dispenser and opened them at the same time, then dumped it all into his cup, letting the pile sift to the bottom instead of stirring it.

"Congratulations," he said. "You deserve it." He emptied the cup and the waitress was there to fill it before he even set it back down. He nodded in thanks.

"So," Nan said, wanting to break the silence, "is your mother the reason you became an oncologist?"

"I'd wanted to do pediatrics. But it turns out I don't have the right interpersonal skills."

"What do you mean?"

"I mean I was suspended for a while. For getting high with a cancer kid in the parking lot. After that I had to choose another specialty. It was strategic really. Oncology was in another building."

"Why would you do something like that?"

"Because he asked me to. And I knew no one else would do it."

Nan's breast began to fizz and pop, as if it had been invaded by electricity. She felt like she could shoot off a firework, put on a show. She could not imagine a life with him; she could barely imagine an evening. But he could help her and for now that was enough. She put her hand on his. He looked down at it as at something recognizable but slightly uncanny, like it was the paw of an animal instead of the touch of a person. "So if I asked you to do something for me," Nan said, "you'd do it?"

When he nodded in return, she felt her left breast begin to sing. The soft thrum did not subside until they reached her apartment.

"Now," she said as she led him into the bedroom, "I'm going to ask you to do something kind of strange."

"Of course you are," he said skeptically. But he made no move to leave.

In a wildly optimistic gesture, Nan had set up the mirror before she'd gone out. As she began explaining what it was he had to do, Dr. Rob did not laugh or even crack a smile. He did not seem to have any outward reaction at all. He watched her with a remote passivity as she began to undress.

When she stood naked before him, Nan worried that he would cast her with a critical eye, that the sight of her body would bring the doctor in him back out. And though his gaze did drift over the scar, when she held out her hand to him, he took it without a word.

She rested her chest against the mirror. It felt at once familiar and brand new against her skin. Down below she could see the single arc of pale pink flesh and the browned and puckering half-moon of her nipple peeking up beside the plane of glass. Beside it stood its spectral twin, steady and simpering and pleading to be stroked. Dr. Rob stood before her and they looked at one another.

"Right here?" he whispered.

"Yes. Right there."

He put his hand on her breast.

At first she felt nothing extraordinary. His fingers on her skin were firm and sure and she tried to concentrate on the throbbing in her right side traveling through the rest of her wilted parts. With each murmur she gave, she tried to give up a little more control, to unstiffen her spine and unlock her shoulders. She shifted her hands from her sides to above her head until her elbows rubbed her ears. She arched her back in tandem with the cycle of his touch.

Then a piercing. Then a tingle. Then a glow built within her. A cautious warmth that crept from them both to meet in her middle. The heat hovered in a spot right above her lungs and her breath escaped her in short, startled sobs. Then it burst above her left chest with the furious flutter of newborn wings. The sensation lasted only an instant but it was so substantial that Nan believed she would look down to find her entire body broken apart. Her phantom breast began to die out along with the flash of light. She met Dr. Rob's gaze, quiet and questioning. But there was nothing to say. She had her first inkling of true loss. And she couldn't get enough.

North Country, Early Morning

They pull up to the hospital in a red car, can't tell the make or year. There's something familiar in them, even after they step out. I'm behind the check-in desk as usual and can see them from the window. They're moving slowly as they make their way across the lot, trench coats flapping in the breeze, clothes underneath dark as a starless sky, so I know it's not an emergency even before I notice the masks. Rubber, I guess; one dark-haired, one gray, but the same jowly faces and twisty grinning mouths. Like the kind you'd see around a cigar.

I seem to understand what they want before they even come in, already turning toward the cabinet and bending over to undo the lock. When I open its doors there's nothing inside. It's empty: just rows blank as children's stares where bottles of pills and syrups should be. And now one of 'em's jumping over the vestibule to stick his gun in my face, the black bag held out for something I can't give him.

"What the fuck is this?" he says, and it takes me a second to realize he's talking to me. That's when I know they're not from around here. Along with their car, their clothes, and the fact that they're robbing us.

As he forces me up, my hands behind my head, elbows sticking out like chicken wings, toward the stock room, he knows the one, he says, I repeat to myself: my name is Grace, my name is Grace, my name is Grace.

My husband, Jerry, talked about grace a lot. Both as a state and an option. "Choose grace," he said. "Be the grace you seek in others." I like this because it sounds easy but is actually something you have to remind yourself to do every minute of every day. Most people walk around the world and connect with it the same way they breathe. That's why it's so hard to change; nobody bothers to think about it.

Sometimes when Jerry called I didn't remember him right away, not until he spoke. He had a bed-making voice. No matter what words he said, his voice smoothed them over like a sheet on a mattress. By the end he'd get something neat and fine out of what originally seemed like a chore. "Choose to be God's grace in this world," he would tell me, "and you will be loved in the next." I wrote that down on a sheet of paper so I wouldn't forget it.

There are six of us on duty between 11:00 p.m. and 5:00 a.m., but only five of us are in the stockroom. The dark-haired guy brings us in one by one while the other stands guard. He holds the barrel of his shotgun pointed down between his legs, as if there's any doubt what he thinks of it, scratching at his chin like he expects a beard to be there. We're all sitting on the ground in a semicircle. Alice and Marie look scared, Kiki looks bored, Ari's wet himself. That leaves Gabe hiding out somewhere. Or wandering around with his headphones on, oblivious to it all. I don't know what I look like.

"Where's the stuff, ladies?" the dark one drawls, the plastic holes that pass for eyes boring into Ari and his damp crotch.

They're all staring at me now, even the bandits. I've been at the hospital the longest, or at least it feels that way. Though I only started working the nightshift after Jerry left, whenever that was. But I don't like that they all seem to know it.

"Deliveries are scheduled for midnight," I say. "They must be running late."

"We could call them," Alice offers. Her eyes have that bunny fou-fou glaze she gets whenever she noses a needle into a vein. "The sheet's by the door."

"Nobody's calling nobody," the gray one snaps. Then he and the other guy go into one of those huddles that criminals are always doing in the movies. Like we won't know what they're talking about.

"What are they talking about?" Ari hisses.

"Shhh," Marie hisses back.

"They're talking about leaving," I say. "That's all." I hope they feel more assured by it than I do.

There's something about this town that you know only after you leave it. That's what Jerry said, at least. He called me the other day from wherever he was. Is everything okay, he wanted to know.

"How long are you going to be gone?" I asked.

He sighed, the sort of sigh you have in the middle of an argument that's been going on a long time. But what did we have to fight about?

"I'm not coming back, Grace," he said.

I waited because I didn't know what else to do, and I'd been doing it long enough anyway.

"You signed the papers years ago, Grace," he went on. "There should be a copy in the rolltop desk in the study."

Conversations like that kind of spooked me, even when I knew deep in my bones I'd had them before. Maybe then most of all. But Jerry was always patient with me, I think. Once he used my favorite lipstick to scrawl "Be Nice" on my vanity mirror. I remembered this because it was still there.

When I went to look for the papers they weren't in the desk but laid out on top of it. As if I'd searched for them already. They were notarized and everything.

The dark one turns toward us and points a finger in my direction. "You're gonna make the call," he says, bending to hoist me up and shoving me toward the phone that's hanging by the doorway. I can feel them all looking at me, or making a point of not looking at me, as I go to the call sheet, find the number, dial, and hold the receiver to my ear.

"Yeah, yeah," the guy says when he picks up, "we're on our way. Got a flat on Route 6. Should be there in an hour. Two at the latest." The sound of a truck passing by is so loud the wind of it almost ruffles my hair.

"We really need you to get here as soon as you can," I say, trying to keep the tremor out of my voice. The gray one's teeth-hugging grin is starting to rattle me.

"Jesus, Grace, give me a break," he snaps.

"I didn't tell you my name," I say.

"I really don't have time for this now," he mutters. Then he's gone.

"Dubya," the dark one says to the other. "Go stand guard out front. And don't do anything fucked up."

"You neither, Nixon," he says, swinging the shotgun over his shoulder as he leaves.

"Guess it's getting-to-know-you time," the one called Nixon says.

Alice whimpers. Kiki rolls her eyes. Ari and Marie just sit there, gripping their knees to their chests, shoulders rubbing like kindling. Somewhere up above is the squeak of a chair on linoleum. Everyone's chin snaps skyward.

"Just a patient," I say. But it's only offices on the second floor.

Jerry said that beyond the borders of our town, past the trailer park, past the toothpick woods and the burned-out cook house by the highway, was a place without forgetting. That he couldn't come back because a fog would settle over his mind once he stepped one foot too far and he wouldn't remember why he'd left in the first place. That it was a miracle he ever did. That was usually when he started talking about God.

"If no one knows what God looks like, He can be in anything you see." That was another one of his I wrote down. But it was hard to recognize Him in the crosses of power lines, in the folds of empty fields, in the methane-bloated faces that surrounded me. "That's your unkindness," Jerry said. "People who only look around the world and notice what isn't there will never know the possibility of the paradise that waits for us."

It's all metal in this room, everywhere you turn. After a while you get to feeling like a piece of food stuck between braces. There's the stale smell of piss in the air, the residue of embarrassment. Nixon's taken a seat on one of the rolling chairs, his gun in his lap, itching at little sandpaper spots on his wrists. Every few seconds he glances up to confirm none of us have moved. We haven't.

"You need some cortisone, Nixon?" I say, nodding at the dark one's flurried hands. "Is that what we call you?"

"Call me whatever you want," he says.

"It's in that cabinet over there."

"Shut up." But he rolls over, rummages around, then finds the green tube.

"I'll have to keep this, now I've touched it," he says, as he rubs the chalky cream into his skin, leaving ghostly prints on his gun, his coat, his mask.

"We won't miss it," Kiki says, snapping the words like gum. It's the first time we've heard from her all night and it loosens the screws in everyone's spine.

"The fuck you ladies do around here anyway?" Nixon asks, surveying the room like he's seeing it for the first time.

"Help people," Alice says.

"Help people," he mimics with lemon-twisted bitterness. I feel sorry for him.

There's a sound then, like a tapping at the window on the other side of the room. We all freeze up, eyes sliding to the floor like children trying to avoid blame. He sits up straight, neck craning. "What's that?" he says.

Silence, aside from the tapping, which becomes more insistent.

Then he's up and stalking quickly over to the window, the wings of his black coat fanning out behind him. We watch him go. He stands on tiptoe, pressing his nose to the glass, the cracks in it catching the light like cobwebs. I can feel my heartbeat in my throat. Marie picks at her cuticles hard enough to draw specks of little bird's-eye blood from them.

"It's just rain," he's saying as he turns and then Ari's up, bolting for the door. There's a flash and a bang, or maybe a bang and a flash. Alice's hands rocket to her ears as Ari stumbles, right knee coming down hard, spit flying from his mouth. Marie is crying, Kiki's eyes are bulging out of their sockets. Blood starts spurting from just above Ari's ankle like water from a hose. I'm getting up to help him when the guy shoots again, at the floor this time, a warning shot.

"Nobody move," he says. His voice is darkness itself, and he follows his own orders.

Most of my days were spent dozing on the couch. There was no reason to be up, really. No sense that I'd missed much of anything.

I made myself something to eat, found a quiet channel on the television, and let myself get taken away on a sea of strange voices. Never the news, full of noise and despair, full of people and places I'd never heard of, things I didn't care to know. I liked those shopping networks, the ladies with their meringue hair, teeth buffed as shiny as the jewelry they held.

Sometimes I'd find the channel with the preacher. Quoting verse, leading a sing-along to a hymn. His arms thrown out, head tipped toward the sky. I fell asleep thinking about Jerry, how something in him just clicked. That's what he was always saying on the phone, that someday it would click for me, he just knew it. The preacher's message was simple and always the same: be better; love one another; don't speak the word of God, just live it. Save another, save yourself.

How much does that need to be said, really? But there was always someone hearing it for the first time, I guess.

"He's hurt," I say. Ari has gone fetal, the blood still dribbling into a purplish puddle beside him, like he's leaking oil.

"He can be dead!" Nixon shouts back. He's in the rolling chair again, hands raking over his dark rubber hair. I can hear him whispering to himself behind the black hole of his mouth.

I try to keep my voice even, testing out the words like water: "It'd be better to let me wrap it at least. Got an awful mess here."

"Shut the fuck up. Let me think."

"You're not thinking," I say, and Alice whimpers, eyes darting between us. "He dies, you'll be in a lot more trouble than you're ready for."

He slaps the side of his head and everyone jolts. But he knows I'm right.

"You. Go get the stuff and bring it to her."

Marie scuttles to the cabinets like a roach not wanting to be caught in the light. She grabs gloves, gauze, iodine, tweezers, needle, thread, and, uselessly, band aids, shoving them all toward me in one tornadic bundle without meeting my eyes.

The bullet's all in one piece but I have trouble keeping my hand steady as Nixon stalks back and forth behind me. I coax Ari into untangling himself, but Kiki and Alice have to brace his shoulders with their knees. All of us are working more from instinct than memory.

Metal nuzzles metal. He moans low in his throat; Kiki claps a hand over his mouth. I worm the prongs inside, grip them around the bullet's sticky body. The cords in Ari's neck strain against his screams. His chest jumps like deer over a field. I clench my jaw, slide it out, the spiteful little thimble clattering to the floor, acting like I've done this before. And now I have. I press the gauze to the wound like a napkin on a dike, thread the needle, make my first shaky stitch.

"Don't pretend like you aren't enjoying this," Nixon sneers. "Even a little bit."

I can feel him close on me, his breath threading my ear, sweaty and thick and missing its whiskey. I want to shake him off but part of me knows there's truth in what he says. I had forgotten what it feels like to be needed so plainly, instead of just doing the needing.

I tie off the stitch and it's done, or at least it's done as it can be. Relief rises in the room like heat. There's not much time left now.

"Why did you come?" I say, as I set the tools aside, peel the wet gloves from my hands. They slump on the floor like animal skins. "What is it you really want?"

He shakes his head. "Don't you remember, Grace?" he says, his voice filled with wonder and pity. "You know what we want. We took it last week. And the week before."

I didn't remember the end of things with Jerry any more than the beginning. One day he was there and he kept being there the next day and the next, each morning waking up to remind ourselves of one another. Until, quite suddenly, he was gone, and then I had to remind myself of that instead. I didn't remember signing the papers either, but it was my signature on them all right. I could see how in some ways, at some times, that might be a comfort. Nobody likes to think about why they might be lonely. I did miss being loved, though, if you can miss a feeling you have no proof of ever having in the first place.

At those times, when I was trying to think up some proof of love in this world, sitting alone on the couch as the morning crept over the land, I would close my eyes and hold out my hands, palms up. A warmth would touch me, reassure me, even if it was just the sun caught by the glass of the window.

"How do you know my name?" I ask.

"I just told you," Nixon cries. He sounds more confused than angry. I can hear his breath heaving underneath the mask, hitting the plastic like a dog's lapping tongue. "We've been here before."

"No," I say, shaking my head, backing away from him, everything else in the room starting to fall away. "No, I think I would remember that."

"How, exactly? Do you even know who Nixon is? You should, you're certainly old enough."

"But *you're* Nixon," I say. "Aren't you?"

He starts to laugh, a secret sound that comes from deep in his body. It's a forgery of amusement, like the sound of the ocean in a shell. Or so I've heard. I've never been there myself.

"Man," he says, "I remember when we first found this shithole. What luck, we thought! We keep coming back here and these idiots won't have any idea! I'm waiting for the day you'll figure it out. Somehow you all know each other," he motions around the room with the gun. "Or at least you can pretend you do. But it hasn't happened for us yet."

Something bubbles up in my stomach. Maybe sick, maybe something else. Either way I swallow it back. Try to stay calm. Now more than any is the moment to stay calm.

"Y'all have a disease, you know," he goes on. "You know that? Of course you don't. You won't remember any of this. Each day the same for you. No worries, no cares, no mistakes. I could even take this off."

He's reaching for his mask when there's a sound far off, a muffled pop-pop like wood collapsing in a fire.

"Fuck!" he shouts, grabbing for his gun.

In that moment, right before we hear the clatter of footsteps then hands pounding at the door, everyone screaming something at once, words bubble up in my head. I don't know where from. Save another, save yourself.

I'm reaching upward; if I could only see his face, his real face, maybe then things would go differently this time. We could both be saved from ourselves, become something to one another. But he ducks from my hands. That's when the door gets kicked in. And we're both turning toward it. Meeting that great white light.

There was a saying I'd been turning over in my head quite a bit since Jerry left, whenever that was. Not for any particular reason, except in my line of work it was a good thing to keep in mind: death is for the living and not for the dead so much. I heard that once, but now I can't remember where.

Departures

Betsy was checking her neighbor's mail again. Not because Fabienne had asked her to, but because the mailman made it so easy to do, leaving it out on the hall table like that. How else was she supposed to know what was going on anyway? If the people living around her were staying or going? This was how she said hello, good-bye. How she remained a good citizen of the building. It needed someone like her, paying attention.

She never actually picked up the envelopes. Just fanned them out on the tabletop, tiptoeing her fingers along the bills past due, the postcards both goofy and sincere, the letters with addresses written in the desperate scrawl of the far away. It calmed her, this little ritual. Sometimes, after coming home alone, she would imagine there was a stranger in her apartment; she liked to think of the sound of the front door scaring them, giving them time to sneak out one of her windows. No one was ever there, of course. Because she was so patient.

Like with Fabienne. Fabienne was a neighbor you needed to be patient with. She was always skittering about the halls, avoiding her like a pest. But Betsy liked her. Maybe even a great deal. She certainly liked her name: Fabienne. She liked the way it sounded in her head, the way it looked written out. Like on this invitation, for instance. The cardstock thick and gray, the name and address firmly stamped. The letters tight and thin, flashing at her like a semaphore. It was asking to be handled.

Betsy picked it up and turned it over, drawing her nail under the seal in one swift motion. It was so satisfying, how it peeled back in one clean piece.

The card inside had the same heft as its envelope, the same stamped type with a woman's name and two dates. February 12th, 1965, and October 4th, 1997. Four days ago. There was an address, too, for a funeral home. Betsy had seen their ads on television. Their tagline claimed they were "The best rest stop before Heaven," a concept that always brought to mind a bunch of decomposing corpses begging for the restroom key and buying cheap beef jerky. The wake was to be held on Saturday.

There was a note paper-clipped to the back. *Fabienne*, it said in a timid hand, *we hope you'll come. It's been too long. She would have wanted you here.*

Yes, Betsy agreed. Who wouldn't want her there?

A door opened upstairs, followed by the muffled sound of someone searching their clothes for a key. She had probably given the person not in her apartment enough time to get out of it by now. She slid the invitation back into its envelope and then slid it into her purse.

While she was getting dressed on Saturday morning, Betsy listened to the news on the radio. She found the man's voice soothing, as if he was telling a story just to her. Today he was telling her about a robbery that had happened in Charlotte on the 4th at the offices of Loomis, Fargo and Company. It was the second largest cash robbery in U.S. history. $17.3 million spirited away. The suspects, one of whom was an employee of the bank, still at large. The FBI had recently found an abandoned armored van with $3.3 million in cash left in the back. They'd opened a tip line that anyone with useful information could call. The ringleader was already believed to have fled the country.

Of course, Betsy thought, as she smoothed her black skirt over her thighs, what else was there to do but go on holiday? She always dreamed she'd run away to Paris. A name like Fabienne would make sense there. Not like Betsy, the name of something you'd lead around on a leash. And this, this is what Fabienne would wear on a day like this one: the skirt, the black hose, the strand of pearls at her throat. The blouse navy blue, a touch both elegantly surprising and respectful.

Betsy had meant to give Fabienne the invitation earlier in the week. But the timing had never seemed right. They were always just missing each other, Fabienne's door shutting when Betsy's opened, a figure vanishing around a corner or a pair of legs disappearing up the stairs. She couldn't very well give an invitation to that. By Friday night it was still in her purse and what could she do? Fabienne should be there, one way or another.

As she walked into the funeral home, Betsy tried to adopt a confident gait, her heels castanetting over the tile as she approached a woman, gray and somber, standing near the entry.

"Thank you for coming," the woman began, trailing off in search of a name.

"Fabienne," Betsy finished for her, taking the woman's offered hand.

The woman tilted her head back, blinked and then narrowed her eyes, looking at her in the way she always imagined birds looked at humans. Then the skin of her face abruptly softened. "Fabienne, of course," she said. "Vicky's old school friend. All grown up now."

"That's right," Betsy said, smiling gently, reaching her other hand up to squeeze the woman's shoulder. The fluid, assured movements of her Fabienne.

"You look so different," the woman said. "But, then, it's been some time. Almost, what, twenty years?"

"It doesn't feel like it's been that long," Betsy said, and the woman smiled and nodded, her eyes already moving beyond her to find someone else in the crowd. Usually when someone did this to her it was an annoyance, a tender blow. But now she took it as a good omen. A sign that she belonged, could be swept onward just like everyone else.

The viewing had been set up in the next room, a line forming along the far wall. Those who had already taken their moment were sitting in the chairs laid out before the casket. A low murmur filled the air like the spectral space between stations; everyone was either avoiding someone's eyes or staring meaningfully into them. Betsy stood behind a man whose posture had the same curl as his cane, clasping her hands in front of her crotch and bowing her head in a manner she hoped seemed thoughtful.

Though there were several pictures on tables throughout the room, it was still strange to see someone for the first time this way: resting serenely in purple velvet lining, body arranged like a bouquet, makeup layered as an onion. A woman behind Betsy had wondered audibly if the effects of the chemo would show, but there was nothing she could see. Still, she was not the sort of woman Fabienne would be friends with, full-hipped with an excessive stone on her ring finger, where Fabienne was all sharp corners and single. But, then, it did not seem they had been anything for a long time. Betsy bent close enough for the chemical spray in the woman's hair to sting her eyes and whispered, "Hello, Vicky. I hope it's all right that I'm here." There was no answer, of course, but there was no objection either.

Betsy took a seat removed from the others, tears from the hairspray still spangling her vision. Fabienne surely would have some sort of handkerchief and she silently cursed herself for not bringing one along.

She noticed a figure out of the corner of her eye, a hulking blur that seemed to be waving something at her. A man, she realized, whispering to her. She turned toward him but he was already getting up from his chair and coming nearer. "It's Fabienne, isn't it?" he was saying, holding out a white cloth like a handful of food for a small animal. "I heard you and Ms. Cross talking earlier."

"Oh, yes," Betsy said, nodding gratefully as she took the kerchief from him, pinching it to dab at her eyes while he took the empty seat beside her. "And you are?"

He was not quite so large as he'd first appeared, or at least he was the sort of large man who carried himself with care. His shirt tugged at him the way a wife would, though it was clear to Betsy that one hadn't chosen it for him. His hair was cropped close to his head in the manner of someone who kept appointments. His eyes were dark and small; she had to seek them as they sought her.

"It's Stan," he said. Then, sheepishly, "You don't remember me?"

He did not seem the sort of man that Fabienne would have been attached to, romantically or otherwise. His name was too clipped, for one. Not like hers, which rested like something melting on the tongue. Betsy had never actually met any of Fabienne's boyfriends, but once or twice she had glimpsed a suited someone emerging from the front door or dashing up the stairs, a spray of flowers in his arms. They were tall, thin, light as birds and just as apt to take off. Someone like Stan would weigh her down. But perhaps that would have been better for her.

"I'm sorry, I–

"It's all right," he said, ducking as if from a blow. "I lived next door to the Crosses. We used to see each other sometimes. But I've changed a lot. We both have."

"How have I changed?" she asked, emboldened by his humility.

"Well, the last time I saw you your hair was braided. It hung down your back and always knocked against your spine when you walked, which was very quickly. Like you were running away from the world. I couldn't figure out why you were in such a hurry. And I never did, since I never saw you again. Until today."

"How old were we?" Betsy asked.

"Sixteen."

"And now we are much more," she said, gazing off in that way she'd seen wistful people do.

"Do you remember," he leaned closer, his nostrils blooming with held breath, "where you were going that day?"

"Of course. I was going on a trip." Fabienne was always getting brochures for exotic locales in her mail. Pyramids, island cruises, ice fishing expeditions in Alaska. Whether she ever went, Betsy didn't know, but she could imagine her in each place and she fit in every one.

"Vicky talked a lot about the trips you used to take together," Stan was saying.

"That's right," Betsy said, seizing on this piece of biography and building a puzzle from it. Of course they had been close once; of course they only had one another. "Me and Vicky and the Crosses. That was the year we went to Florida. To Weeki Wachee Springs. Do you know it?"

He shook his head.

"It's a state park," she continued. "They have a live mermaid show; that was our favorite part. The girls in a tank, propelling themselves back and forth with artificial tails. They breathe air through tubes that run from small tanks on their backs. We stayed for hours, watched the shows back to back, until her parents pulled us away. But," she said, her voice growing heavy, "that was the last trip we took together."

She glanced up then, checking his face for cracks in the story he'd just been told. But he was still, his gaze resting fully, comfortably on her own. He was listening to her, she realized. But not just to her; he was listening for something inside her as if at the hollow of a tree.

"Do you still travel?" he asked.

"I dream of it. But my work keeps me here. I manage a department store." It was sophisticated but not flashy, exactly what Fabienne would be. Betsy was a receptionist for an insurance company; she spent all day repeating, "And who shall I say is calling?"

She could be so open with this man. Anything she gave him he accepted.

"And what do you do?" she asked. A Stan like this one must be something sturdy but dazzling, high-wire with a net underneath. An attorney, a physicist, a pediatrician.

"I'm an accountant," he said.

Stan stayed by her side through the speeches. They laughed when everyone laughed and looked sad when everyone looked sad. He stayed with her as they got up and made their way toward the exit where Ms. Cross stood once again, clutching the hands of people as they passed. It seemed only natural; surely men were always following Fabienne around without being asked. Affixing themselves like barnacles to a ship.

"Fabienne," Ms. Cross said when they reached her, "it was good of you to be here. And Stan. Vicky would have been happy to see you two together again."

"I'm sorry it's not under better circumstances," Stan said, pressing Ms. Cross's offered hand in both of his.

"Me, too. Fabienne, would you mind waiting just a moment? There's something I need to speak with you about." Before Betsy could object, before she could even think about wanting to, Ms. Cross was linking her arm through hers and leading her down the hall to a darkened room.

There was nothing in the room except several chairs with coats thrown over them like an assembly of ghosts, and Ms. Cross motioned for Betsy to sit where she pleased. She remained standing, head down, concentrating on the wrinkled lacing of her fingers. Her avoidance of Betsy's face shot something cold through her. For the first time that day she was worried.

"I'm not quite sure how to say this," Ms. Cross began. "It's not easy for me."

"You don't have to," Betsy said, preparing to rise, to leave before being asked. But Ms. Cross held up a hand to stop her.

"I didn't like the idea of the lawyers handling this," she continued. "It seemed crass. Better it be kept among family. And I hope you still think of yourself that way, Fabienne. As family."

"Of course," Betsy whispered, thinking of Weeki Wachee Springs, where they had never been. She had seen it on a postcard once, though, sent to someone else.

"Anyway," Ms. Cross said, turning to wrestle something from the pocket of her blazer, "Vicky wanted you to have this. It's not much; she didn't have much to give. But it's what she wanted. Something about paying back what she owed." She held out a piece of folded paper, turning discreetly away while Betsy opened it, as you'd do for someone undressing. A check for five thousand dollars made out to Fabienne.

"Thank you," she said, folding it back up and slipping it into her purse.

"Yes, well, I have to get back out there," Ms. Cross said, turning to leave her before pausing at the door. "Please, Fabienne, come and see us sometime."

"I'd like that," Betsy said, but she was already gone.

Stan was still waiting for her in the hall, which made her anxious. Betsy didn't like people being around her when she had to think. She could feel the check settling in her purse, weighing her down like the actual bills it promised. She had never had this much money before, not all in one place. She feared it might make her a little reckless.

After all, there was no way she could give it to Fabienne now. There was no adequate explanation she could offer. Nor did she want to think one up. She was the one who had come, out of the goodness of her heart. It was important to Vicky that she have it. What good would it be for Fabienne to know about it, since it was hers now?

The question was what to do with it. She would not be able to take it to a bank; for one thing, they would all be closed at this hour. Nor could she see much point in saving it, letting it molder away in the dark recesses of some metal depository, at the mercy of middle managers and thieves, while she went back to living her old life. Surely Vicky would want it better used than that.

"Is everything all right?" Stan asked, shifting forward onto the balls of his feet as she drew near.

"Fine," she said, and laughed in a way she hoped seemed offhand. "I've just come into some money, in fact."

Something dark passed over his face and just as quickly disappeared. "Oh? I hope this doesn't mean you won't let me take you to dinner."

But Fabienne would not be afraid to ask for more than that. Fabienne would take a risk. Indeed, she would be waiting for moments like this, to become what she was meant to be.

"I think," she said, turning to let him fold her coat around her like a pair of arms, "you'd better take me to the airport instead."

They stopped by his office first, where she endorsed the check in Fabienne's name, and he gave her a stack of bills from a safe by his desk. It seemed so small in her hands, no more dense than a deck of cards being held together with a dingy rubber band. She felt burdened by it, now that it was something she could see, could hold. Money always looked so ugly up close. It was no wonder those bank robbers left a whole truck behind.

"You don't want to stop anywhere else?" Stan asked as they got back into his car. "Your place, maybe? To pack?"

She thought of all those nobodies not in her apartment, not making themselves at home. "There's no point," she said. "I'll just buy what I need there."

To her surprise, Stan chuckled. "You always were mysterious. Like, for instance, how you've managed to live here all these years and we've never run into each other."

"Maybe I didn't want to be seen."

He shook his head, but in that downward way people do when amused. "You know, I tried to see you. A few years back."

Betsy stiffened, let her right hand rest on the door handle. But the car was already in motion, the houses and gas stations and drugstores of her town waving good-bye.

"I wasn't looking for you, I swear," he continued, keeping his eyes on the road. "I just stumbled across your number and address. Called a couple times. Never got an answer. So," he cleared his throat, "I went to your apartment one day."

She remained silent, waiting to hear what he would say about her.

"You were wearing a bright yellow coat when you came out. I was parked across the street. I meant to get out and say hello, but there was something in your manner, the way you walked, that made me stay where I was. You kept your head down, even when people passed right by you. You seemed so closed off. Not at all how I remembered you. Not at all how you are now."

"That wasn't me," she said. "I don't own a yellow coat. You must have seen my neighbor Betsy. From a distance we look a little alike."

Stan chewed at his lip. Outside the buildings had fallen away, replaced by forgotten fields, vacant lots, the detritus of civilization that often scattered near places people went to get away from the place they were.

"I guess it's good I didn't do anything, then," he said.

"What would you have done? If it had been me that day?"

"Well, I would have acted surprised to see you. And pleased. And you would've been pleased to see me. Maybe we wouldn't have embraced. But we'd have shaken hands at least. I'd have said I was in the neighborhood, asked if you lived around here. You'd have laughed and pointed at the building behind you. I'd have said that I interrupted you on your way somewhere, but you'd have invited me to walk with you. Maybe you would have been on your way to work at the department store. I'd have persuaded you to stop somewhere for lunch or a cup of coffee. And we'd have sat and talked. About all the things that had happened since we were kids. Where we'd been. What we'd seen. I'd have told you that I'd been married for a few years. And that I see my daughter every other weekend now. How I don't love my job but I do love my work. How I look forward to fishing on the weekends. How every once in a while, when I'm out in the boat and nothing is biting, you'll cross my mind and I'll wonder what you're doing at that moment. You'd have laughed when I told you this. And taken my hand. Before we'd part we'd have agreed to do it again sometime."

"That sounds like a nice day," Betsy said, as Stan pulled the car into the airport lot. She knew it was just a story and not even one meant for her. But she wanted to be a part of it. It was better than any day she'd ever had, this day that had never happened.

As he reached for the gearshift, she placed a hand on his forearm. "Let's have it in Paris," she said. "It's what Vicky would have wanted, after all. After all the grief she put us through. Heaven knows," she laughed, thinking of Ms. Cross, how resolute she seemed thrusting her daughter's money into her hands, "she owed us more."

"Is that how you remember it?" Stan said. His gaze had a sour twang to it like a wrong note struck on a string, reverberating through his features. It startled her, this dubiety, and yet when she reached for his hand he gave it. Indeed, the confirmation of her flesh seemed to soften him. He put the car in park.

It wasn't until much later, after they'd bought their tickets, gotten through the line at security, and were comfortably in their seats as the plane began its ascent, the little houses outside the window growing as small in sight as they were in her esteem, that Betsy thought about what would happen if they crashed. What God she would call to, what she would say, who she would say she was. For surely whatever was left of her would not be identifiable as Fabienne. Not that it would matter to whatever was left of Stan.

It was already getting difficult to tell what below them was land or sea.

Stan reached for her hand, and she rested her head on his shoulder, the movements so fluid and natural between them it was as if they'd been making them all their lives. Perhaps they had been, or at least were preparing to. This was her reward, for being a patient person. She could wait for such a long time.

Lookaftering

Louisa hadn't even realized she was pregnant when she gave birth to the eggs. She woke up late, after Wally had left, and so made her own breakfast. As usual when this happened she didn't care for it. She felt fine while scraping the leftovers into the trash, but later, while lying out on the couch, she began to feel a strange uncoiling in her stomach, like a snake letting loose from a trick can.

Wally found her that evening, standing over the toilet.

"What is it," he said, in that flat way that didn't want an answer.

"I'm not sure."

There were three of them, each one about the size of a fist, pale lilac in color. They'd made a dainty plop when they hit the water, sliding down to gather together in the crotch of the bowl.

"What the fuck, Louisa," Wally said when he came to stand beside her.

"Well, this is just as much your fault as mine," she said.

"Whoa, now," he took a step back, "let's not go throwing words like that around."

"They got inside me somehow."

"Don't look at me," Wally said. "Anyway, I thought you were on the pill."

"I'm on *a* pill," Louisa said.

She crouched down, wanting to get away from him for a moment. The eggs were still; their shells showed no cracks from knocking against the porcelain. There was something peaceful about them.

She wondered how heavy they might be, how delicate. There were so many others she had cracked thoughtlessly over the years, little white shards in her wake. She reached down and picked one up.

"That's it," Wally said. "I'm outta here."

It settled in the center of her palm, the same weight and texture as a billiard ball.

"Aren't you going to help me with these?" she asked, to his departing backside.

"Are you snake or bird?" she shouted to the empty doorway, but he did not return to her. Not for a couple days, at least.

By then Louisa had done her research. She'd dried the eggs, wrapped them in a dishtowel, and set them underneath her desk lamp, which she kept lit at all hours even though it made it difficult to sleep. Her fourth-grade class had done the same with chicken eggs for a group experiment once; she'd been the only one to see them hatch. They'd come out wet and wobbly, like chewed-up gum with a pair of legs. None lived more than a couple days. Six years later, in high school, she'd had to carry around a sack of flour for a day, treating it like an infant. When she wasn't looking, one of the other girls had cut a hole in the bag. The next time she picked it up white powder spilled all over the floor. Louisa was determined to do better this time.

Wally liked to make dramatic re-entrances into her life, so she didn't bat an eye when he tumbled through the door, hair mussed, clothes polluted, the smell of lost spirits on his breath. She was seated at the kitchen table, one of her mother's old encyclopedias propped up in front of her.

"Did you know," Louisa said, as he began banging around in the cupboards for the coffee, "that the female platypus, after mating, will construct an elaborate underground burrow from leaves and reeds to house her eggs? She drags these materials to the nest using her curled tail."

He sniffed the grounds he found, made a dissatisfied grunt.

"And," she continued, "that the female platypus doesn't have teats. Milk is released through the pores in her skin."

"Please, Louisa," Wally said, "I can't handle this right now."

"But you will later," she said, looking up at him. "Or else you wouldn't be here."

He didn't answer her then, but that night, reaching for sleep as one does for air underwater, he rolled over and put his hand on top of hers and squeezed.

Louisa and Wally had been living together only four months but they'd known each other since college. She suspected it was because of these two combined factors that he came back to her, despite his reservations about the situation. They both were twenty-seven now, and though they had once professed to grand plans for the future, they both worked part-time. He tended bar on weekday afternoons or, as he called it, the graveyard shift. She had been a receptionist at a gym but was fired two weeks earlier after mixing up Krav Maga and Capoeira, inconveniencing two trainers and thirty students. "It just doesn't seem like you care enough about the Crush Fitness family," her boss had said.

She and Wally had never discussed having kids before. That was still something that only happened to other people, like parents with cancer or getting accepted to graduate school. They were pixels on a Facebook page. They were decisions, or at least accidents that became ones. But surely parenthood was not the word for what this was. Surely there was some other way to make sense of it.

A week went by, during which the eggs didn't seem to change at all. Louisa wanted to keep them in the kitchen because it was the room that got the best light. But that seemed reckless. And what would they do if friends came over? They never did, but still.

Instead, she built a nest out of shredded old newspapers, adding a little more every day as the world carried on its own business. When she held them in her hand she swore she could feel a tiny pulse inside.

Then one morning Wally announced, "I called your mother."

"Oh God," Louisa said. "She's not coming down here, is she?"

Her mother had a house four hours away by car but had never been to visit. This was how she made her disapproval of their living situation known.

"She thinks you're being irrational and wants you to see a doctor."

Louisa rolled her eyes.

"I think it's a good idea," Wally said.

"Maybe I should see a vet instead," she grumbled. But she knew he was right.

Luckily, Doctor Sparks had an opening that afternoon. "Did you know," Louisa said on the drive over to the offices, "that parrots nest in cavities, like tree hollows or cliff sides? And that both parents participate in the excavation? There's often intense competition for spots. When the babies are born they don't have feathers."

"I really don't think you've laid parrot eggs," Wally said. He'd insisted on bringing them along; Louisa held them in her lap, stored in a Tupperware container lined with cloth napkins.

"I know I haven't," she said. "Parrot eggs are white."

"Plus, they live over a hundred years. I wouldn't want our kids to be around that long."

Louisa smiled; Wally always joked like that when he was nervous.

"Well," Doctor Sparks said, after Louisa had positioned herself on the exam table, slapping his hands and rubbing them together like he was hovering over a steak dinner. "What seems to be the trouble?" She had been going to Doctor Sparks for six years, but she still never felt entirely comfortable around him. He had a bald head and a tall, thin frame, like a beaker turned upside down, and a jovial, forthright manner that she found irritating. She suspected he couldn't be trusted to deliver bad news.

"Hmm," he said, after she explained what had happened. "Maybe it was something you ate," and directed a barking laugh at Wally, who was seated between the sink and a box of toys meant to distract young children.

"I think this is pretty serious," he mumbled.

Doctor Sparks cleared his throat, chastened, perhaps, or merely disappointed. "You have them with you?" he said, turning back to Louisa, who handed over the container. He popped it open and picked one up, holding it to his right eye while closing the left, spinning it with the counterfeit expertise of a pawnshop owner appraising jewelry.

"Any lingering discomfort? Or spotting?" he asked.

Louisa shook her head.

"And while you were passing them, did it hurt?"

"Not really," she said. "It kind of felt like sex. But in reverse."

Nobody knew how to respond to that.

He listened to her chest through a stethoscope, prodded her stomach with his fingers, offered to send her down the hall for a sonogram, but Louisa declined.

"I can't find anything wrong with you," Doctor Sparks said.

"Well," Louisa replied, "I guess that's a relief."

They were both silent on the drive home, at least until they pulled into the apartment building lot. "For the record," Wally said as he eased the car into its space, "I didn't think anything was actually wrong with you. I just wanted to be sure you were safe."

"I'll be sure to note that down in my 'Pro Wally' column," she said, pinching him affectionately on the upper arm.

That night she fell asleep listening to phlegm rattling like a sticky marble in Wally's chest. It sounded like growing old together.

A week later Louisa answered a knock at the front door and found a reporter for the local news station standing there.

"What do you want?" she said, more curious than malicious.

The woman was young, perhaps as young as herself, and she seemed as tightly wound as her hair. She'd matched her nail color to the shade of her blazer and skirt so meticulously that Louisa found herself staring at her, wondering which decision had come first. The woman stared back, waiting for her to notice the camera crew that stood behind her and the puffy-headed microphone she held close to her breast.

Wally was at work and usually much better at turning people away from the apartment, so she didn't realize what a mistake she'd made until they were inside, eyeing with unkindness the unframed concert posters on the walls, the loose screws in the Ikea furniture, the stacked dishes listing in the sink. "May we see them?" the newswoman asked. She'd introduced herself. Her name was something alliterative, but Louisa had already forgotten it.

"See them?" she repeated.

"The eggs," the woman said. "They are real, aren't they?"

Louisa winced as if threatened with a blow.

"Tell me," she blurted, "are you familiar at all with the emperor penguin?"

Later that night, when the segment was airing, the eggs looked dull, dishwater gray, neglected in their large, shabby nest. The light from above reflected on their surfaces like tiny windows, the camera moving steadily closer until they nearly filled the screen, grainy and utilitarian as a missing person's photograph.

"Do you sit on them?" the woman's voice asked, before the view cut to Louisa propped on the same living room couch from which she watched now with Wally.

"Do I look tired?" she murmured, reaching up to touch her face. But Wally shushed her: "I want to hear what you say."

They stared at her funhouse mirror image before them, waiting.

"No, I don't," the image said. "I think the weight would be too much for them."

"Was that a good answer?" Louisa asked. Wally shrugged, keeping his gaze on the television.

"What do you imagine is inside them?" the woman asked.

"I don't know, but I hope they look like me."

"Would you call yourself their mother?" she prodded.

"I think I'll wait to hear what they want to call me."

Wally laughed. "That's a good one," he said. There was a beery glint in his eyes that Louisa didn't like the look of.

"You know," the woman continued, "many parents struggle to prepare even for one child. What are you going to do with three?"

"I think I'll manage," Louisa's image said. "Lots of women deal with much more."

"So you're raising them alone then?"

Onscreen Louisa shrugged and the camera cut abruptly to the outside of the apartment where the newswoman stood, a veil of grave concern over her features. She began intoning about absentee fathers and single mothers, the scourge of unplanned parenthood on the land.

"Wait, they cut me off!" Louisa said. But Wally was already getting up from the couch. "I said you would be helping me. I said they could find photos of us on the fridge. I took them in the kitchen and showed them. I told her we were like emperor penguins, how the female transfers the egg to the male after she lays it. How sometimes during the process couples drop the egg and the chick inside freezes. I told her we wouldn't be like that. We'd be like the ones who recognize one another's calls."

"It doesn't matter, Louisa," he said. "You should never have let them in to begin with. Why? Why did you do that? Why did you show or tell them any of it?"

"Because she didn't believe me."

"Who cares?" Wally spat.

"I needed her to believe me," Louisa said. "We can't be the only ones who believe."

Wally shook his head, stalked into the bedroom, and shut the door. The news had moved on to the weather. There was a week of sunny days ahead.

There weren't many of them, at first. Just a few neighborhood ladies with hair the color and style of cotton candy peeping through the front windows. When Wally saw them he rapped the window with his knuckles, as if to scatter them like birds. But they returned the next day, and the day after that, growing in number each time.

"What do you think they want?" Louisa would ask, but Wally was still not speaking to her, at least not directly.

One day after Wally left for the bar she ventured out to them. Some had brought lawn chairs and sat knitting or flipping through magazines; others loitered further back, leaning against the railing that rounded the property. When Louisa stepped out they all turned toward her in unison, like creatures in some nature documentary. She paused in the doorway, waiting for one of them to say something. But they were waiting too.

"Can I help you?" she asked.

The women exchanged glances of covert import. "No," one of them said. "We're here to help you."

"That is," said another, "we want to be *of* help."

"We saw you," another said, "on the news."

"You seemed lost," shouted one from the rear.

"That boyfriend of yours, always coming and going," the first said, and the others shot her disapproving looks.

Louisa regarded them with curiosity. The older women in the building had never shown much interest in her or Wally, never responded to their greetings with more than a nod or a curl of the lip. Their youth marked them as interlopers, freeloaders, reminded them of the worst impulses of their own kids, who threw water balloons at the mailman and got arrested for trespassing at the railyards. But there was an amusing quality in how they gathered, mobilized, as if maternity was something that must be bestowed.

"Let me think about it," she said.

That night Wally came home tripping over the tips of his shoes.

"Did you know," she said as he tumbled into the bedroom, "that snakes use internal fertilization? The males store paired, forked hemipenes in their tails that hook into the females' insides."

"Ouch," Wally said, but it may have been for other reasons.

"They also abandon their eggs as soon as they're laid," she continued. "Except for pythons, which coil around them until they hatch. Female pythons will even shiver to generate heat for incubation."

She got up from the bed and went to the desk, plucking one of the eggs from the nest. The lilac color had begun to fade, as if it'd been left too long in the sun; now it looked the same dishwater gray as it had on the television.

"Do you think I should do something else with them?" she mused. "Maybe build something that will keep them on my person? Like a pouch or a sling?"

"You're doing fine," Wally slurred. "You're doing fine lookaftering them."

Louisa held the egg up to her ear as if she might hear the ocean in it. But there was just the gentle swell of Wally's snores.

Once, not long after she and Wally started dating, Louisa was approached by a lost girl in the mall. She looked exactly the way you'd expect someone left behind to look: saddle shoes, pigtails, thumb in mouth. "I can't find my dad," she'd whispered, giving the last word clear uppercase emphasis, when Louisa bent down toward her outside the Orange Julius.

Louisa did everything she thought she was supposed to do. She asked what her dad looked like. He was tall, thin, wore glasses. He was a doctor, which was a fact provided without prompting. She let the girl lead her by the hand around the stores while she conveniently remembered that no, her dad hadn't come in here after all. Louisa tried locating a security guard but the girl always distracted her with tears or a request for some of her soft drink. Finally, after the girl asked to use her cell phone, Louisa gave her all the money in her wallet and left her by the fountain.

"You did the right thing," Wally said when she told him. "I'm sure it was a scam. I bet her dad wasn't even a doctor at all."

At the time Louisa convinced herself that she agreed, but now the memory frightened her. It seemed some sign of her capacity for monstrousness.

A week after the women began to arrive, Louisa's mother called. "I saw you in the grocery store this morning," she said in her brittle-boned voice. A life-long smoker.

"That's impossible," Louisa said. "I haven't been to the store."

"Not *you*. Your face."

"My face?" Louisa repeated.

"You're a tabloid sensation," her mother said, with the same enthusiasm she reserved for announcing the results of a recent colonoscopy.

"I am?"

"Don't speak like that, honey. It makes you sound slow."

"But I don't understand what you're telling me."

"You're on the cover of *Idol*. There's an article, too. About you and Wally and your little . . . situation."

Louisa glanced over at the eggs, as if they might have heard.

"Well? What about it?"

Her mother sighed, which set something loose and she began coughing.

"Now, honey," she continued once it passed, "I've known Wally for years. You know that I love him. But."

Louisa waited.

"But it just doesn't look right. Him never being around, coming home late, drunk. It's all in the story."

"And?"

"Don't you see? Everyone who reads it will think they know things about you. Like the way they think they know things about movie stars. Or the president. Or anyone who's not them. I just want you to be prepared, that's all."

Louisa sighed, raking her teeth along the edge of her right thumbnail. "Do you remember those encyclopedias you gave me?"

"Not really," her mother said.

"It doesn't matter. But I've been reading them. Most fish, you know, engage in oviparity. The females lay a great number of eggs, sometimes several million, which are externally fertilized by the males. Then the eggs are left to develop on their own. The parents have really no say at all."

"True," her mother mused. "But how many end up as caviar instead of fish?"

After hanging up Louisa went to the front window and peered through the curtain at the women outside. Most were doing what they had been doing all week: chatting, painting one another's nails, taking lopsided selfies. But a few held copies of *Idol*, were shuffling through the pages, the image of the eggs from the television reproduced in queasy close-up, like quivering porno flesh. Louisa shrank from the sight. She wanted nothing to do with them.

Wally found her on the bedroom floor in a fetal curl around the nest. He knelt down and held a copy of *Idol* in front of her face.

"How did this happen?"

He didn't sound angry, only deeply, deeply sad.

"The way all of it happened," she said. "Without anybody asking me."

"Nobody asked me, either," Wally said, bringing his butt down and crossing his legs to sit.

"I did," Louisa said. "On the very first day. I asked if you would help me."

"And I am. Aren't I?"

Louisa sat up, rubbing at her eyes, blurring the Wally before her.

"Is this what you think of me?" he continued. "What these rags say?"

Wally came back into focus. He looked older than she remembered either of them being. She thought back to when they had first met, which was different from when they first decided on one another. It was at a party in college, held in an abandoned apartment complex. Half the roof had already been torn down and the rest of the building was set to follow in the new year. The first snow of the winter came early and the floors were covered in a damp white dust. There was no electricity; everyone huddled around trash can fires, or one another, for warmth. Others sprawled out on the staircase that led up to an open sky. Beer was retrieved from a bathtub filled with ice.

They'd gotten into a room upstairs somehow, underneath a shredded section of the sky. It was empty aside from the snow, which had fallen in haphazard clumps from the jutting skeleton of the roof. The wallpaper had split and peeled away in the cold; it hung from the walls in stiffened strips, like a woman caught undressing. The floorboards groaned beneath them as they wandered. "Is this safe?" Louisa had asked.

"Probably not," he said.

He'd tried to kiss her that night, but Louisa, skittish and virginal, took one step back too many and fell to the ground. She lay spread-eagle for a moment, not sure what to do. Then she brought her legs together and her arms down and made a snow angel.

Later Wally would confide that was the first moment he knew he could love her. She couldn't remember when she knew she could feel the same way.

Now Louisa reached out for the paper and began tearing off pieces, adding them to the nest. Wally watched her in silence until she finished, little black smudges left behind on her fingertips. Then he grabbed her left wrist. He held his other hand out, palm up.

"Do you trust me?" he said.

Several years later, after Louisa had given birth to their first child, while Wally was out trying to locate some coffee in the hospital commissary, two nurses waited while she tried to get her new daughter to latch onto her breast. It was a tedious process to watch as it was almost always successful, eventually, and yet it kept them in a state of suspense nonetheless. The baby's head lolled about like a buoy on an ocean.

"She'll get it," the younger one whispered to the other. But the older one was not convinced. How could you ever know a thing like that?

Now Louisa reached into the nest and picked up one of the eggs, then placed it gently in Wally's outstretched hand. It was the first time he had held one. They'd grown no larger in their six weeks of existence but there was a density to them now that felt fibrous, braided, less like the pulsing of a heart than the flexing of a muscle.

They held their breath as Wally let it settle into the cradle of his palm, both looking down at what was between them. As the minutes on the digital clock ticked silently by, they drew closer until their foreheads rested one against the other, forming a chaste tent. Then, just as they were starting to get comfortable, there was a tiny cracking sound, like kindling starting to splinter in a fire. Something was breaking through the surface of the egg. They remained as still as possible, waiting to see what they had made.

THE WORLD TO COME

Those Who Left and Those Who Stayed

The night the ground beneath Sherwood, Alaska split in two, the only witness to the tragedy was Kirby, the village drunk. It was mid-December and the kind of cold that cracks cloth. In summer the earth was damp and suckled at the townspeople's toes as they walked over it. By winter it was always brittle, temperamental, sharp as elbows. Anyone with a bed was buried deep in it.

As the floe broke loose and began to float away, carrying nine of them with it, Kirby slumped against a lamppost and watched the shoreline recede slowly into the darkness. No one, as usual, heard his hiccups.

They lost the lights first. Then the rest of the electricity followed. At three days in they were storing perishable food outdoors. Kirby downed the remainder of his alcohol, then stepped off the ice and into the sea. Two more tried to swim back to shore. Another vanished trying to find the other side of the floe in a storm. The five who remained moved on to the canned and dry goods. The youngest was seven, the oldest eighty-three, and the rest were somewhere in between. Before they had been neighbors. They weren't certain what they were now.

With no reception and all lines cut, most of them lost hope of getting in touch with loved ones left behind. But they held on to wild possibilities, of passing a steamship or getting picked up by a helicopter traveling overhead. Maybe a whale would swallow them whole, turn them into a colony of Jonah's. Or maybe they'd plow right into another piece of land. Eventually the hope of being rescued or perishing in such ways dwindled too.

Lloyd, the town handyman, was the first to wake on the morning after the split. His first thought was to find his flashlight and shine it over the sea in the hope that someone would answer. He had a fiancée, Orya, back in the town. She'd been living with her parents until they could marry. Everyone agreed it was the respectable thing to do. But the glow was too slight to meet anyone; it disappeared into the jaundiced fog. Lloyd never realized how ugly the sky could be when it was all you saw.

The second thing he did was take a hatchet to his front door. He'd been building a raft ever since. He was a man who needed something to do with his hands.

When he and Orya first met, he had asked what her name meant and she said peace and that was what she would give him. This had been true for a time. But the last few weeks he'd been dreaming of other women's faces. It would happen unexpectedly, while he was sanding down a board, for instance. He'd bend over to pick up the stray curls and suddenly there was a woman beneath him, one he hadn't thought of for many years, her hair tangled in his fingers, her body warmer than anything for miles.

He couldn't think of his fiancée this way, though he wanted to. They had not yet known each other in the intimate sense. This was Orya's bidding; she was nineteen years old and, having waited this long, perhaps didn't see anything disagreeable in waiting a bit longer. Lloyd obliged because he was thirty-four and still somewhat surprised that she had agreed to know him at all.

He remembered her spider-leg eyelashes. How she read cookbooks all the way through, like a novel. He thought how well she'd taken to his mother, Beulah, and feared what they spoke of without him there. He imagined her standing at the ocean's edge, in the wedding dress he hadn't yet seen her in. He wondered how long she would wait to leave him. That was when the images of others came in: the soft down belly of one, the violin-bowed body of another. Moving beneath him, above him, and then wriggling out of sight, as they had in his life. He used to see them walking in town. They'd smile at him in that knowing, pitying way. Almost all of them married other people the year after they'd been with him.

Lloyd continued to build, taking the post office, the bar, and its swinging saloon doors along the way. Though few words had passed between him and the others on the floe, it was assumed he would take them with him. The construction was slower than he hoped; he hadn't worked without electric tools since his apprentice days and the labor of it exhausted him.

Jude stopped by daily to check his progress and ask for firewood. The boy was seven and caught here with his mother, Alicia, one of the many women from the cannery who mourned a husband that still lived. The boy must have sensed Lloyd's fatigue because one day he invited him to have dinner at his mother's house. The offer touched Lloyd. He had never been entirely comfortable around children; they made his already hulking figure seem perilous. But on his way over that night he caught a glimpse of Alicia undressing through her bedroom window, lit up by a pauper candle. Her belly was full and indulgent as a yawn but even from a distance he could see her skin had begun chipping like ice, the dark hoods that had settled under her eyes. As he watched, she slowly worked a comb through the ragged net of her hair. The somber beauty of it clanged his bones and, rather than eat with this woman and her son, he turned back around and sent his ax through the door of the bookshop. The force of it rattled the pages that hadn't yet frozen together. Jude continued to visit him, but he never extended the invitation again.

Alicia was running out of food to feed her son. One morning it was six dry flakes of cereal in a milkless bowl. Would the next be sawdust? Milk from her own breast? If there were any animals, she'd hunt for them. But out here each crunch across the ice could echo for miles, a single step made seismic. It seemed they were alone.

Her son was not a good eater and over the past few weeks Alicia had been making a game of their meals, splitting up his food into real estate. Plots of peas, mashed potato complexes. But there was not enough here to make a single home. She'd already stopped eating just about anything herself.

"It's not good to skip breakfast," he told her once.

"I'm not hungry," she lied.

Jude reached across the table for her bowl, tipped his sideways, and parceled three flakes from it to hers. Then he pushed it back without a word. They ate them one at a time, letting the cereal melt into soggy cardboard on their tongues.

She tried to maintain some sort of normalcy with Jude, sending him off during the day to spend time with Ms. Kimball, the schoolteacher. She wished him to continue learning, even if it were things he wouldn't be able to use.

Her husband, Espen, had never put much stock in education. He'd dropped out of high school when his father died to take his place in the family whaling business. They married not long after Alicia graduated. In Sherwood there were two strains of romantic desperation: that of the young, to find someone, and that of the old, who didn't. Divorce was rare but a match made wisely was rarer.

Espen was not a bad husband when he was there to be one. But his work often kept him from home and Alicia was unprepared for the loneliness that would come to blight her love. She spent her days working in the cannery, wearing the prints off her fingertips, and her nights knitting sleeves that never evolved into sweaters. When she slept she fantasized about the other men in the factory pasting mermaid-shaped labels onto her skin; when she laughed the mermaids shimmied like tattoos. Espen would crash through the door unannounced, a shock of salt in his beard, offering a vial of ambergris or a soapstone sculpture, and Alicia would feel the surface of her heart split like a cold lake. She tore at the layers of his clothes as if she hardly believed the body underneath. When she had their child, she didn't know where to wire the news. Now they were both at sea, though she suspected he wasn't trying to reach her. With so much more ocean to sail, he had no reason.

Drifting apart. What an inadequate way to describe people deciding to leave one another. As if all it took was going limp. Every night Alicia sat down at the table with Jude and again neglected to tell him about his father. After so many days working in the factory, she had longed for such closeness with her child, but now she didn't know what to do with it.

On the morning she and Jude split their flimsy breakfast, Alicia resolved to do better. She gathered herself into her warmest coat, went to the closet where her husband stored his things, and dug out his fishing line and tackle box. She hadn't been angling since she was a child but the howling of her stomach thwarted the demurrals of her head.

Alicia hadn't been outside in weeks; looking out over their limited land, the houses that were left seemed to huddle together against the wind. She wasn't certain how long she walked until she reached the floe's edge, but it didn't seem long enough. The ice simply dropped into the sea, like someone turning a corner. Today the waves were calm, a sort of dirty-dish gray, but she could recall the nights when the water sounded like it was preparing to knock on her door, vampirically awaiting an invitation to come inside.

She must have sat there for hours, drawing the line through the water, casting and reeling nothing back. The lure bobbed about the surface like a child at play. She remembered the catches her father would return with, heaps of fish, the scales shining like treasure. Her mother would fry them in a pan with butter. They would freeze the rest until winter and then roast them over the fire along with chestnuts. But this sea betrayed no life roiling beneath it. She was right: they were alone.

That night she dreamed again of the sea, the waves seething, parting, unhinging like a jaw, leaping up to swallow them whole. She woke in a flood of sweat. In the morning she took something else from her husband's closet: a rope, which she instructed Jude to tie around his waist and attach to the front doorknob before he went outside. An old trick farmers used on their cattle in storms. She would not lose another man to these waters. Not yet.

Ms. Kimball was a teacher with no schoolhouse. For twelve years she had been teaching twenty students in a single room at Sherwood Junior High. Some of those students would never take another class after hers. Every fall she gathered up her composition books, bundled her pencils, clapped her erasers clean. Every spring she counted down the days until she returned. The purpose had been ripped from her life. She had expected it to happen much sooner.

Sherwood had two kinds of people: those who left and those who stayed. That was all the town was. Ms. Kimball was unique in that she had come to it. For a time after her arrival she had been the object of great speculation among the other residents. She was a woman whose smallness was often thrown into relief by her solitude; she stood out from the town like a lonely nesting doll. Perhaps she was an escaped inmate on the lam. Or part of the witness protection program.

The truth was Ms. Kimball was fleeing nothing more mundane than the sort of depression that the wealthy cured with insurance-proof pills. When she was thirty-three and living in Santa Fe her fiancé had left her for a man who taught civics in a neighboring district. Several hours later she was found at the local grocery store, wandering the baking aisle, slitting the bags of sugar like throats. She was quietly asked not to return to school the next year.

In the first few days on the floe, Ms. Kimball attempted to adjust to her new isolation. She broke into the bookshop and stole all the Harlequin romances. She joined Kirby for a couple belts on the bottles while he was still with them. She went to Mr. Ruben, the elderly invalid she had never seen on dry land, and listened while he played his records. Flashes of her former gloom would visit her, urging her toward a darkness more absolute than night. When Alicia came to her, asking if she would tutor Jude, she accepted partly in the hope that the boy would keep a bad something at bay.

Five weeks in Jude was beginning to look frail. Or at least she thought it was five weeks; she'd stopped crossing the days off her calendar once they'd passed the New Year. On the walk over to Mr. Ruben's, hands clasped, stepping on the ice with the unpracticed gait of topiary come to life, Jude told Ms. Kimball of his wish to go to the moon.

"What's on the moon?"

"Don't know. It just seems weird up there. I'd like to go somewhere weird."

"More weird than this?"

It was strange to walk over land that stayed the same as far as the eye could see. It was what, as a child, she'd always imagined the clouds of heaven to look like. Yes, how different was this from the moon, really? They had about as much chance of being heard and even less of being believed. Then she stumbled over a rocky patch and gripped Jude tighter. Their hands were almost the same size.

They entered Mr. Ruben's house without knocking; he never answered anyway. His communication was rigid and tidy, restricted to gesture, the glottis, and his record player, old enough to be cranked by hand. He was a widower, had been for as long as Ms. Kimball had lived in Sherwood. They were there to keep him company and feed him, if he wanted it. Sometimes he did. Sometimes he let the soup dribble down his chin.

Mr. Ruben was in his chair, a mound of blankets at his feet that Ms. Kimball quickly picked up and arranged on his lap. It was colder here than it was outside. Around them the walls wolf-whistled; the clapboards were stacked and gappy as unbraced teeth. A frost had formed on the kettle and it took several matches before she could get the wood in the stove to catch.

"I took a trip once," she said, pulling the kettle from the flame. "To India."

"Not possible," Jude said. This was what their lessons amounted to now: she told him of her life and he pretended to be interested.

"This was a long time ago. Before the floods came."

"What was it like?" Jude asked.

"Hot. Always hot. You couldn't get away from it, even in the shower. You couldn't really get away from anything. It's funny, now I can't even remember the last time I sweat."

She poured the boiled water into a mug and dipped a dusty tea bag inside, carrying it all to Mr. Ruben, who didn't move to take it from her.

"Did you see any camels?"

"Once or twice. I saw all sorts of things: palaces, snake charmers, bodies laid out in the street. I watched a missionary perform an exorcism. I even bartered for a pair of sandals in bare feet once."

"Must have been sad to come back here," Jude said.

"Yes, but it was necessary. Half the appeal of a journey is that it won't last. The way back is always shorter than the way there."

She lifted the mug to Mr. Ruben's lips and was rewarded with a hasty slurp. As she pulled away, she felt that old creeping unpleasantness she thought she'd left in New Mexico. Perhaps it was the talk of India. Perhaps it was the boy and his candlewick face. Regardless, she knew that the creep would soon turn to a sprawl and she would do something cruel.

Jude heard once that there were places where animals were kept stuffed behind glass, twisted into poses that made them look like they had in life. He'd never seen it himself. His friend Freddie had gone on vacation and come back with tales of standing so close to beasts he could fog up the glass between them with his breath. It felt that way now, being stuck on this ice. But who was watching them? Maybe God, but Jude didn't know much about him either.

All his life he'd been dreaming of things he'd never seen. For as long as he could remember his dreams, he'd imagined stowing away in the hold of his father's ship and waking up on the same land he did. But now that a true adventure was at hand, he didn't know how to enjoy it.

Partly it was his mother, who was shrinking from the world in ways he didn't understand. He had always accepted her as beautiful, in the way women in fairy tales were beautiful; it was less about how she looked than about how men held doors open for her or how his father used to gaze at her from across the kitchen table, a comical glint in his eye, as if contemplating the plank of wood that kept him from the woman he crossed an ocean for. Now her growing weakness frightened and angered Jude. He knew it wasn't her fault, but who else could he blame? Every morning when he pushed half of his cereal toward her, his resentment, a feeling he knew but couldn't name, thickened.

Six weeks on, one of Jude's teeth came loose. He was poking a finger through a hole in his favorite shirt, trying to tickle himself, when his tongue lifted his front incisor from its root. It hung suspended for a moment then flapped back into place. This didn't concern him immediately; he'd lost teeth before. But this one was full grown. His father had pulled it from his mouth over a year ago.

Before leaving the yard, he tied the rope around his waist and attached the other end to the front doorknob. As he picked his way over the bald expanse of ice, the growls of his stomach were matched by the whip of the wind and the snow enveloped his footprints as soon as he planted them. The rope flopped behind him like a misplaced cowlick.

Jude enjoyed these excursions despite their difficulty. On his seventh birthday his father had promised to enroll him in the Cub Scouts. Jude began making his bed drum tight every morning. Once or twice his mother humored him by bouncing a quarter off it. That summer she'd even let him sleep outdoors, draping a sheet over a low-hanging branch to make a pup tent. He traced the stars out with his fingers, dreaming of the day he'd know their names. That was almost four months ago and he hadn't seen his father since. He didn't know the stars any better now, though he saw them more clearly out here; they seemed closer, too, as if the sky was sinking.

Halfway on his journey he stopped to say hello to Lloyd, who was outside working on his raft. The rope followed behind, nipping at Jude's ankles like a dog. "How is it?" he asked. He still hadn't gotten used to speaking easily with Lloyd. The man's hulking presence and quiet manner had always frightened Jude; he took up space without warning. But now Jude was glad Lloyd was with them.

"Not bad," Lloyd said, stepping back from the plane of wood as if to admire it. "Think it could hold about seventy stone."

"How many stones do you need?"

"Don't know. How much is your mother weighing these days?" His mouth was smiling but his eyes were limp.

Jude didn't knock before entering Ms. Kimball's house, a lapse in propriety that made him feel oddly adult. She called out his name from the living room, as if it could be anyone else. The sound of it bounced off the bare walls. A few weeks ago there'd been a painting in the foyer, a woman with dark skin, long braids, and no clothes. Jude asked about it, then it disappeared.

In the living room he hesitated to approach the woman sprawled out on the couch. Her face was tucked into the crook of her arm, her breath straining to escape her. She reminded him of a man he'd once seen while walking in the woods with Freddie. The man had hair like knotty black string and fingernails long enough to curl. His eyes couldn't seem to settle on anything. He wore a bracelet on his wrist, white and plastic, and when Freddie stepped on a branch as they ran away, they heard him let out a low moan. That night the police swept the area but Jude never came across him again. Ms. Kimball looked like that man, except he actually knew her, which made it all the more frightening.

"Do you think the ocean ever gets tired?" she mumbled into her hand. "It's been going since the world began, you know?"

Jude didn't quite know how to respond to an adult who wasn't looking at him.

"Always carrying the rest of us on its back," she continued. "Where do you think it's taking us now?"

"Home?"

"What home? Maybe Siberia. We can be prisoners too."

"I want to go home," Jude said.

She turned on him then, the thorny mass of her hair, her uninhabited eyes, her jaw wound tight like a music box before it sings. She looked poised to pounce and Jude jumped backward, stumbling over an unplugged lamp cord.

"Go, then, what's stopping you? Nothing, that's what. There's nothing there."

"My father's there."

"Your father left your mother months ago. That means he left you, too."

"No," Jude shouted. In the hurry to get the word out, he almost pushed the tooth loose.

"No?" Ms. Kimball said. "Ask her. Just ask her. Nobody's there. Nobody's anywhere. We're alone. We're more alone than I thought it was possible to be."

Then she deflated like a balloon, collapsing back into the couch in a silent heap. Jude watched her for a moment, his pulse jangling in his head, a fire building on his fingertips. He glanced at the cord at his feet, the lamp attached to it, and the rope attached to him, coiled on the floor like Eden's snake. Then he turned around and ran.

The wind hit him like a bear hug, a huge enveloping gush of air that almost pushed him back into Ms. Kimball's house. For a moment he saw nothing and felt a surge of blind, furious hope. When his sight returned he still saw nothing. Just white upon white upon white. It buried whatever else he was feeling.

Lloyd was not at the raft but the ax was. Jude didn't lift it so much as throw himself behind it. The blade ripped through the wood, sending splinters raining through the air. His tooth was knocked from its socket with the effort and as he spit it into the snow, a jerky piano rang across the hill. And then a voice tiptoed over it. Mr. Ruben had put a record on. *Baby, won't you please come home.* The same record every night. With the taste of blood like a penny on his tongue, Jude readied himself for the next blow.

The boy would be forgiven. Boys always were. Until they were men and not so easily worthy of forgiveness. Then old age came and they could be pardoned again. Mr. Ruben would know. He'd been them all, once.

Mr. Ruben had lived every one of his eighty-three years in Sherwood. Some he remembered better than others. Since the death of his wife, Zuleika, eleven years before, he'd been trying to forget the rest. Not that he had loved her so very well. Mr. Ruben was a man who always thought hard about being better. He just never seemed to find the time to do it.

The year Mr. Ruben was born was the hottest on record. This excited his parents, who believed it portended something great for their son. Then it kept happening year after year. A new record, a new disappointment. Soon enough, a new everything.

Here's what he understood about Jude: there was a great confusion to being young, a frenzy that most adults were more than happy to forget. Every single thing was the biggest yet. His own memories of those days were culled objects, like a museum show of his own making. There was the bucket his mother used for fresh well water. If he drank directly from the ladle, he received a scolding. It must be poured into a glass instead, the liquid so clear and sharp it popped when it hit his tongue. He remembered his first and only lobster, its hard red shell and the sound of it splitting, like a bad word you couldn't take back. Watching his father shoot a reindeer and two weeks later giving his mother the pelt for Christmas.

He watched the town sputter through history, growing and receding and going gray. Every few years another upheaval: the fishing industry failing; the young people migrating; the winters colder and shorter, feral and blunt; the summers hanging on like bated breath. As a child he'd been taught that March was in like a lion, out like a lamb, that April showers brought May flowers, but such sayings dropped out of use by the time he was in high school—they no longer met the needs of the new world. He lived a life not much different from that of his parents: he married young, worked until he was sixty, haphazardly raised children of his own. If they were occasionally wanting for something, there were always neighbors to help. The things he was used to having he eventually got used to doing without.

Since Zuleika had passed, he'd stopped listening to anything aside from his records; he read no news and heard from no one. So perhaps the town's misfortune had been inevitable. Perhaps they'd stayed too long in a place they shouldn't have. It had surprised but not alarmed him to wake up one morning floating on ice. Though he did feel bad for the young people, he couldn't help being delighted at this last excitement of his life. He had expected to drift off into the ether of old age; now he would meet a great and unusual end. He spent every day with salt kinking his nostrils and the current beneath his feet, tugging him further into a world muted enough to write his last wishes on. He didn't have many.

The teacher had promised to stay with him. For years he'd exploited his own deficiencies, allowed everyone to believe he was worse off than he was. The world in his head had always seemed better than anything anyone else offered. Perhaps for her he could lay the charade aside.

Here's what else Mr. Ruben understood: life was a series of big moments and by the end you could forget every one. Each night when he nestled into his chair and put the needle down onto his Bessie Smith record, he did not think of Zuleika or his children or the town he'd left behind. Instead he saw a darkness, much like the one that surrounded him now, and two friends he hadn't seen in many years, boys again as was he. They had smuggled themselves over to the house of their history teacher, Ms. Ratched, and were lifting one another to look into her window. The others had come back down with nothing to report, but when he had his turn, she was there, stark naked, standing in the middle of the room. Her body was taut and still slick with water, the skin stretching over her like a grape's. A cigarette dangled from her fingers, the ash floating carelessly into the carpet. Over by the unmade bed a pair of black high heels awaited her return. The three of them squealed and ran together, and it seemed in that moment that there was nowhere they couldn't go.

On the morning they pushed the raft from the floe, a fog unrolled itself over the ocean. Lloyd could barely see his own hand in front of him, but he didn't think that would keep them from getting somewhere. It had taken another two weeks to repair the damage that Jude had done. It might have taken less if his mother hadn't made him help, sulking while he drove the same nails into the same plane of wood. They were huddled together somewhere nearby, though Lloyd couldn't see them either. They'd grown so thin the wind must have been cutting through them like clothes on a line.

Neither Ms. Kimball nor Mr. Ruben came to see them off. Lloyd expected this. But Mr. Ruben didn't play a record for them either. This disappointed him. Now that they were going, he could admit it might be the last song he ever heard.

As the floe became a mound and then a white line and then an inkling, a fear gripped him, coarse but not unpleasant. A fear like presents at Christmas. A fear like something coming apart in space. A fear like the day when he was twelve and running along the edges of Sherwood with his friends and was the first to see it: a whale, beached on the open palms of the land. The scent of fish heads and formaldehyde was in the air. Even from a distance they could tell it was still breathing; they watched the labor of it work across its body. But they were young and selfish and kept it a secret. Two days later it had grown solid with death and yet no more real. They went closer and then closer until it was as big as an eclipse. They dared one another to be the first to touch it. Lloyd was the second; it was damp as a fevered forehead but without the relief of warmth. In the end the National Guard had to airlift out the corpse via helicopter. No one had seen a creature on shore since.

There could be no music waiting for them. There could be nothing at all.

As the sea bent beneath them, a beat entered his brain: Orya, he thought. Orya. And whatever hopes were in the heads of the others joined him in turn. It became the current they were crossing.

To order or obtain more information on these or other University of Nebraska Press titles, visit nebraskapress.unl.edu.

CPSIA information can be obtained
at www.ICGtesting.com
Printed in the USA
LVHW09s1633240818
587910LV00006BA/479/P

9 781496 207876